My Boss and I

Enemies to Lovers

J. D. Hova

J. D. HOVA PUBLISHING
JDH
WHERE IDEAS COME TO LIFE

Table of Contents

Chapter 1

WALTER:

$\mathcal{M}$y heavy footsteps slapped against the ground as I jogged down the tarred path that led to my estate. The sun's golden rays just began to peek from a lazy morning cloud, but I was already soaking wet with sweat from running 10 miles within the past hour.

My heart pounded rapidly, with every beat echoing in my ears like a distant drum over the Beethoven music blasting through my headphones.

"Almost there…" I huffed, each breath felt deep and satisfying, but the lungs still craved more air to replenish the oxygen-depleted cells. His teeth grinding against each other as he drew closer to the gate.

My calves stung like a thousand bees were feasting on them, and I knew they had turned an unhealthy shade of red, but I didn't stop. The pain sent a wave of adrenaline through me, fueling me with strength and a weird thrill of satisfaction.

I know what you're thinking. You think Walter Wolfhard is a strange man, but you are right, and I am well aware of my eccentricity. I don't mind my unusual quirks and weird fetishes as long as no one is harmed. In fact, I celebrate them.

Maybe that was one of the reasons my ex left me. Pretty messed up, but on the bright side, I'm glad she did go. She called me a crazy psycho just because she did something that was supposed to 'hurt my feelings,' but I didn't give her the satisfaction she wanted.

Okay, she cheated. So what? What was I supposed to do, cry myself to sleep? Please, I had better things to waste my time on. Did I love her? Maybe. Was I hurt that she cheated? Not one bit.

They say honesty is the best policy, but your judgy eyes make me wonder if you want to hear the truth. Maybe you won't look at me with those eyes if I lied instead. Meh, just kidding, you don't have enough willpower to break me.

You know what? Maybe Chantelle was right. I am crazy.

Besides, building a successful empire in the heart of a metropolitan city takes a level of madness.

The silver gates of the Wolfhard Estate slid open as I inched close to it. The adrenaline dissipated slowly, and my quick steps soon turned into a brisk walk.

A hiss escaped my lips as I crouched under the searing pain that shot through my muscles.

I shouldn't have attempted to complete a 10-mile run in thirty minutes. Mopping the sweat dripping down my face with the towel hanging from my shoulders, I made my way towards the front porch, where Hubert stood, waiting for me with a tray of drinks.

"Good morning Sir, I–" Hubert's hoarse voice greeted, and I held out my hand to silence him as I gulped down the glass contents.

The last time Hubert broke the terrible news while I was drinking, I ended up in the Emergency Room. The fact that he doesn't seem to have learned a lesson from that experience makes me wonder if he was just dense or if it was all part of his plan.

"Sir Walter, there's–"

I shot him a long, hard look, enough to shut him off in the middle of his sentence as he swallowed hard.

My tense muscles instantly relaxed as I chugged the drink, and a sigh of satisfaction escaped my lips. The day was going well, and I thought I could get through the morning without falling into a sour mood.

I spoke too soon.

"S-Sir..." Hubert began, shuffling after me as I walked down the hallway to my room.

"This better be important, Hubert." I deadpanned, but a female voice interrupted before Hubert could say another word.

"Good to see you're still in good shape."

I sighed, turning around to face the woman who birthed me.

"Mum." I said with a tight smile. "It's great to see you."

"Of course you are; look how excited you are about my visit." Mum replied with sarcasm. Now you know who I got it from.

The smile on my face widened, and with arms open wide, I walked over to the dotting woman in front of me.

"Don't even think about it; you stink!" She shoved me away, walking towards the adjoining balcony. I knew she expected me to follow her, so I did. The city was already awake, with the distant sound of traffic cutting through the serenity in the air.

"You're here so early. Is everything okay?" I asked as we both took our seats.

"Well…" Mum grunted as she lowered herself to sit.

"I knew if I didn't come by so early, I would miss you, and you know I can't just stop by at your office to discuss this."

"Discuss what exactly?" I arched my brow in confusion.

"You, Walter," Mum said, with all traces of humor gone from her voice.

I exhaled, running my hand through my hair.

"Mum, please, can we not—"

"Ellie called." Mum dropped the bomb.

"She said you broke up with her."

"Well, she cheated, and I asked her to go have some fun." I shrugged. "And not come back here, of course."

"Wasn't that your fault?" Mum scrunched her face in disbelief. "Why are you acting like this? "

"What did Eleanor tell you?" I frowned. "Tell me what she said to you."

"That you cheated, and she was hurt, so she didn't know when she did it," Mum replied.

"Yeah, right, I bet it was an accident. She tripped and fell on a dick. "

"Walter!" Mum warned. "Did you or did you not cheat?"

"If she meant I spent much time at work instead of traveling the world to watch her runway shows, I did." I shrugged.

Mum blinked in confusion. "Excuse me?"

"Wait, you didn't ask her what she meant by 'cheating,' did you?" I snickered. "She meant I cheated on her with my job."

"T-That…Is interesting." Mum stuttered, visibly struggling to process the new information.

"Of course it is." I deadpanned.

"Look, mum, I know Eleanor. She's trying to get you on her side, but you can tell her I'm not interested." I said, rising to my feet.

"Walter, why don't you hear her out, okay? Take her calls, at least." Mum rose to her feet as well, following after me.

"I'm not a dog mother, and I can't return to my puke." I drawled.

"Ew, come on, Eleanor is not puke." Mum retorted. "She's just a good girl who… made a few mistakes."

"I do not have the luxury of time to listen to whatever she has to say, Mum. Time is money, and that activity brings me zero cash." I sang, clearly uninterested in what Mum had to say.

"Walter…"

I stopped in my tracks, turning to see my mum's eyes well up with tears.

"Mum…please don't do that." I sighed, walking up to her.

"Why do you care so much about Ellie anyways?" I asked her, wiping a stray tear that dropped from her eyes.

She scoffed. "Who cares about Ellie? I want you to settle down with someone and be happy, Walter. "

"Here we go again." I groaned, turning around to climb up the staircase.

"Walter, you're 36, and I'm not getting any younger either." Mum followed after me. "You should consider settling down soon, you know."

"Right." I drawled, my patience running thin. The woman who birthed me is one of the few who could get on my last nerve.

"Walter, don't walk away from me." She called after me, but I just waved at her.

"Bye mother, thank you for stopping by."

"Walter!" Mum's fading voice echoed as I slammed my door shut.

HAILEY

The sound of monitors beeped rhythmically, which I have gotten used to since my mum's accident a few weeks ago.

Tightening my grip on my sling bag, I walked into the ward, where my mother slept soundlessly. The only sign of life I clung to for dear life was her chest's steady rise and fall as she took in purified oxygen through her breathing tubes.

"Hey..." I whispered, gently running my knuckle down her cold cheeks. The heaviness in my chest intensified, and I swallowed the sob fighting to escape from my trembling lips.

"It's day 25...and I just want to let you know that I miss you... so much..."

My voice betrayed me at that moment, faltering with every word.

My mum was everything to me. Since Dad left, all we had was each other. The day of the accident still haunted me every time I closed my eyes to sleep. She had called me to let me know she would be working late. I was at my friend Stacy's when she called, just doing regular girl stuff.

Life was so normal, and then suddenly, it wasn't.

When I got the phone call from the hospital that Mum was in a bad accident, it felt like my world just came crashing down. Mum was working two jobs, and I was yet to apply for any job here in Chicago because I was waiting for a response from the colleges I'd applied to.

Seeing Mum covered with so much blood was mortifying, leaving me with nightmares for days. With Mum in the hospital, I knew the bills needed paying somehow, so I had to take up a full-time job to take care of Mum and the bills that weren't going to pay themselves.

I looked up at the wall clock across the room, and my eyes bulged out in terror.

"Shit!" I jumped to my feet, dashing out of the room like my feet were on fire. I was running late again, and I knew I was in trouble.

I jumped into the car, and that was when the old piece of junk decided not to want to start.

"No, no, no, no!" I repeatedly cried out, turning the keys, but there was no sign of life.

"Piece of shit!" I screamed angrily, giving the car one last kick before running out of the parking lot to flag down a cab. Tears threatened to spill from my eyes as I waited impatiently for a taxi to stop by, but none was in sight. Fear choked my heart, and pictures of me clearing my desk after being fired crossed my mind.

That was enough to add springs to my steps as I broke into a run, my tangled curls flying against the wind. I didn't care if I looked crazy as I dashed across major roads with tears running down my face.

I couldn't afford to lose this job, so I knew I had to do what I had to do. Wolfgang stood tall, with the sun reflecting off its grey glass windows. I dragged my aching legs and sweaty body through the gigantic gates, my heart slamming against my chest.

I took a peek at the parking lot, my eyes wandering in search of a familiar blue Tesla, but it was nowhere in sight, and I sighed in relief.

I snuck in through the back door, trying to act as natural as possible with my limp curls and sweat-soaked blouse. Ignoring the blatant stares from my colleagues, my mission was to arrive at my office without getting caught by the CEO.

As I walked down the last hallway, my eyes darted about, on the lookout for him. I sighed in relief when I walked into my office, glad I could escape his wrath that morning.

Unfortunately, the universe seemed to be playing a sick joke because I had taken my seat when the telephone rang. The shrill sound of the old junk made my heart skip a bit, and I eyed the ringing telephone warily.

With trembling hands, I reached out to take the call, slowly bringing the telephone to my ears. I sucked in a deep breath before speaking.

"Hailey Hernandez speaking, how may I help you?"

I bit down hard on my lips as I waited for the person on the other end to speak.

"Hailey, come to my office...now." The familiar baritone I dreaded filled my ears.

Chapter 2

HAILEY

With trembling steps, I made my way to Mr. Wolfhard's office, fear clinging to me like a second skin. The closer I got to his office, the more my stomach twisted into a thousand knots.

I hated that damn place. Every time Mr. Wolfhard summoned me, something went wrong, and a punishment was waiting for me.

The shiny oak door with a golden crest of a wolf towered over me, and I gulped. I was in trouble for the third time this week, and I had no idea what awaited me at the other side of the door.

"Oh fuck it." I gritted my teeth, cracking the door open with my sweaty palms to reveal the lush interior which led to Walter Wolfhard's office.

I locked eyes with Tanya, his obnoxious personal assistant who hated my guts for reasons I didn't understand. Today wasn't different, even though she had a knowing smile tugging at the corner of her lips, mocking me.

She seemed to know what fate awaited me, but I hid the fear which consumed me a little too well. It was a battle of will as I shot her a stern glare while holding her haughty gaze.

I couldn't let myself fall apart in front of Tanya, so I looked away from her and headed straight to the door at the end of the room.

I landed three knocks on the giant oak door, biting down on my lips as I anticipated his response.

The door slowly cracked open, and I walked into the lion's den with quivering legs. The familiar dark interiors sucked me in as I made a beeline to the mahogany desk at the center of the room.

He was seated behind the desk with his eyes glaring down at me.

I stopped at the foot of the desk, staring straight into his hawkish green eyes as I swallowed a whimper.

"Ms. Hailey Hernandez." My name rolled out of his mouth with a wisp of venom, making the hairs on my skin stand at attention.

"Sir." I forced out, trying to keep my voice as firm and professional as possible, even though all I wanted was for the ground to open up and swallow me.

"What time is it?" He asked, his stubble chin resting on his intertwined fingers propped up on his desk.

"Um..." I stuttered, my words failing me. The last I checked was when I was still at the hospital, so I genuinely had no answer to his question.

"Turn around." He commanded, his voice jolting me into action. Without thinking, I turned my back towards him as I stood face to face with the giant wall clock in front of me.

"Now, Hailey, tell me what time it is." His voice was low and lethal, and I interpreted the time on the clock with wide eyes.

"Five minutes past eight," I muttered, guilt laced in my voice.

"Louder."

I clenched my fist, sucking in a sharp breath as I repeated.

"Five minutes past eight, Sir!"

"And what time are you supposed to be at the office?" Mr. Wolfhard asked.

"Eight O'clock sharp." I replied, knowing what was coming.

"Hailey, this is your second strike this month." Mr. Wolfhard said, leaning back on his ergonomic chair.

"I apologize, Sir." I replied.

"I don't need your apology; I need you to work on yourself." Mr. Wolfhard continued.

"There is no place for slackers at Wolfgate, so next time this happens; we might have to ask you to go."

My heart skipped a beat at his last words, and I tried not to break down in front of him.

"Now, for your punishment…" Walter rose to his feet, taking slow, predatory steps toward me.

"Since you like storage rooms so much..." He lifted the golden key dangling between his fingers. "You're going to take this key and sort out all the files alphabetically."

Son of a bitch!

I wished I could say that out loud, but all I could do was murmur a feeble response.

"Yes, Sir."

He scoffed. "Not like you had a choice anyways...if you want to keep your job, that is."

My heart sank as I considered the stress of looking for another job. I had to do this...for Mum.

"Think fast!"

Without warning, Mr. Wolfhard tossed the key, leaving me to grapple with the air in an attempt to catch it.

"Tsk, Tsk, slow as a sloth..." Walter shook his head, walking away to take his seat. "I still wonder how you got hired in this organization.

Those words stung like a bee, but they weren't the cause of my worries.

The real problem was the key.

Where did the damn key go?

I scanned the marble floor for any sign of a golden key but returned with nothing.

"Sir...I can't find the key." I said.

"Not my problem." Mr. Wolfhard shrugged, his eyes still locked on his computer screen. "Why don't you search for it, Ms. Hernandez?"

When he wasn't looking, I shot him a dirty look which was enough to convey the words I couldn't say. How did he expect me to find a key that was nowhere to be found?

"Well, what are you waiting for, Hailey? Search for it." Mr. Wolfhard's voice interrupted my thoughts. I bit down on my tongue till it bled, right before crouching on my knees in search of the missing key.

After several minutes of sweeping the floor with my dress in a fruitless search, a soft clink caught my attention; behold, the key was right in front of me.

Tears stung the corner of my eyes as I took in the smug look on Mr. Wolfhard's face.

"Run along now, no need to thank me."

A painful whimper escaped from my lips as I nodded, slowly rising to my feet.

"Hailey." His voice stopped me in my tracks, and I balled my fist in fury.

"Yes, Mr. Wolfhard?" I gritted my teeth.

"This must be completed today, along with your daily task. Is that understood?" Mr. Wolfhard said, and I nodded, half-running out of his office.

———

WALTER

What's worse than having your mother fuss over you like a child? It's having your assistant inform me of information I couldn't care less about.

Except it had to do with the recruits to the firm, of course. There's no way I would let them disregard my company's ethics, not on my watch.

That is precisely why I had much fun dealing with Hailey Hernandez.

I had no idea how she ended up in my firm in the first place, but since she stepped in, I've had to deal with her case repeatedly.

Watching her run out of my office with tears brimming in her eyes brought an indescribable thrill of satisfaction. After starting the day on such a rough note, it felt good to do something that I enjoyed.

Call it tyranny if you want, but I didn't become a CEO by being spoon-fed and coddled like a baby, so I will not treat my staff differently.

They work for me, and the door is wide open if they are not ready to abide by my policies. We get enough applications to fill an entire storage room.

I might add the exact storage room I had sent Hailey to sort.

After Hailey walked out the door, Tanya walked in with a tray of coffee and desserts.

"I noticed you were in a sour mood, Sir, so I thought to bring you some coffee and cake to cheer you up." She said in a sultry voice, her lips lifted in a seductive smirk.

"How sweet of you, Ms. Genova," I mentioned, lifting my eyes to take in the seductress in the guise of my assistant.

"I must say you look outstanding today, Sir…" Tanya said, inching closer to me. I noticed her skirt was a little shorter than earlier in the day, and I wondered if she would ever stop trying to hit on me.

"Thank you, Tanya Genova; as you can see, I'm working now…" I pointed to my laptop sitting on my desk. "But I appreciate the coffee and cake, even though you're just doing what I pay you for."

Tanya didn't seem to appreciate my sarcasm as her smile faltered.

"You may leave now, Tanya. And ensure you ring me before coming in here unannounced. I've warned you several times before."

"I apologize, Sir." Tanya curtsied, hesitating for a moment like she was expecting something more.

I kept my eyes glued to my screen, not sparing Tanya a glance, and she took that as her cue to take her leave.

"You're sure you don't need anything else?"

"Tanya…" I warned, narrowing my eyes at the lady trying to hard to get my attention. At first, it was cute, until it became plain annoying.

"Right." She muttered before shuffling out of the office. One of my guilty pleasures was watching her bum wiggle as she went. She was pretty, alright. But I didn't want her to get too comfortable even though I returned her flirty advances sometimes.

Tanya left, and I was finally left alone to continue with work. Several hours passed in a blur, and soon it was time for a lunch break.

The telephone rang just when I was about to leave the office, and I sighed in exhaustion. As much as I wanted to let the phone ring out, I'm still haunted by one telephone call I missed, which led the company to lose a high-paying budget to our competitors.

I wasn't going to take any chances.

I walked back to my desk to take the call, only for my ears to get hit with the disappointing sound of Tanya's voice.

"Tanya, it is lunch break. What do you want?" I asked in exasperation.

"Um, I'm so sorry, Sir. I just called to remind you it was lunch break so you could take some time to rest..." She drawled, "And...I also wanted to know if you would like me to get something for you from the food court?"

"No, Tanya. Thank you very much." I slammed to telephone down before storming out of the office. Walking down the deserted hallway, the only sound that filled my ears was the rustling of papers from the storage room.

I walked over to where she worked, leaning on the door frame while watching her.

"It's lunch break." I finally spoke, only earning a sharp look from Hailey.

"Come on, I might be an asshole, but I'm not that much of an asshole to steal the only hour you have to rest from work." I continued, walking down the path she created in the storage room. What used to be littered with papers now had a clear way from Hailey working tirelessly through them.

Hailey had successfully arranged most of the papers on the wall shelf and was about to tidy up more of the floor.

"Thank you, Sir." Was her curt response, her back turned towards me while she continued shuffling and arranging papers. Did she tell me off?

I frowned, pressing my back against the wall shelves stacked with papers.

"It wasn't advice, Hailey. It was an order."

She stiffened, her hands hanging in the air as she was about to place a stack of papers on a shelf.

"You also 'ordered' me to complete all tasks due today, Sir. I would not be able to achieve that if I took a break." Hailey replied with pain and anger sipping out of her voice.

"Hailey." I called her. "You obey the last command. That's the universal military rule. "

"I didn't know Wolfgang was a military base." Out came Hailey's sarcastic remark. Her mop of blonde curls shielded her face, but I could feel the sneer in her voice.

I knew she was mad about the punishment, but I wouldn't break protocol to assert dominance.

"Don't make me repeat myself, Hailey Hernandez."

She turned around, eyes brimming with tears.

"Fine!" Her voice quivered. "I'm just…trying my best to do the right thing, but I guess you're never going to stop making my life here a living hell."

I arched a brow in confusion, trying to figure out where she was going with this.

"Well, thank you for letting me take a break." She sighed. "I hope it won't be used against me in the end."

She spared me one wary glance before dashing out of the storage room, leaving me perplexed.

HAILEY

I wiped the tears from my eyes before they fell, trying to maintain my composure as I walked into Smallie's, the Cafe across the street from Wolfgate. I could have quickly gone to Wolf's Den, the company's cafeteria, which served free food and everything, but I didn't want to be surrounded by people who hated my guts.

The free food wasn't worth the crippling anxiety that awaited me there. I would have ended up losing my appetite anyways.

After the morning drama with Mr. Wolfhard, I knew I had to leave that building before I lost my damn mind. I needed to breathe a different air, so with the time I had left, I headed to the cute Cafe right across the street.

Smallies was my comfort space, where I could be by myself and relax without worrying about the multiple pairs of haughty eyes boring holes into me with hate.

At first, I'd thought it was because I was still new at Wolfgang, but it's been almost a month, and the awkward atmosphere still lingered. That was when I knew there was something more to what they let on, causing me to feel so poorly.

I never really stuck around long enough to find out. My first day at Wolf's Den made me feel like a deer walking into a den of lions. I could feel their eyes boring holes into my skin, and I had to bite down hard on my tongue to stop myself from bursting into tears.

For the first time, I heard rumors about me, making me want to claw out my ears. I spent most of my time at my desk, doing everyone's job, while all they did was surf the internet and watch funny videos. What time did I have to fool around with anyone?

At first, those rumors offended me because I worried they would fall on the wrong ears, but I disregarded their blatant lies. There was no need to defend myself; the CCTV cameras could do that for me.

As I walked through the doors of Smallie's, the sweet smell of pastry filled my nostrils, and I inhaled a deep breath. Relief washed over me when I looked around and noticed no recognizable faces among the few persons having lunch.

"Hello," I said with a wry smile as I reached the counter to place my order. There was a girl around my age and two guys who were busy with some orders. I'd seen her several times here, but for the first time, I checked her tag, and it said her name was 'Nina.'

Her smile was bright and wholesome as she walked over to me.

"Hi Curly, What are you having today?" Nina asked.

Reflexively, I tucked some strands of my limp curls behind my ears with my fingers as I placed my order.

"I'll just have…a hamburger and an iced latte please."

"Coming right up, pretty lady." Nina winked at me, and a shy smile crossed my lips.

"Thanks; I'll be at the third booth at the back." I pointed out before taking my seat while waiting patiently for my order.

It was always pleasant to have Nina take my order. She was the most excellent barista I've ever met, and sometimes I wondered how she always stayed so cheerful.

Deep down, I knew she was one of the reasons Smallie felt homely for me, even though I'd hardly admit it.

I pulled out my phone for the first time since morning, checking for any messages. Life has been so different since I finished high school. All my old friends were off living their best lives in new cities where they went to college, and I was just…here.

With only a few messages from a college group chat I'd joined in high school and one spam notification, I sighed.

My social life was a mess, and I had no energy to fix it. All that consumed my mind was work and getting my mum back on her feet again, and the thought that she was still fighting for her life made my eyes sting with tears.

"Order up!" Nina chirped, walking towards me. I wiped my eyes furiously at the sound of her approaching footsteps to get rid of any trace of tears from my face before she arrived,

"Brunch is served!" Nina sang, almost twirling away, and I couldn't help but burst out in laughter. With little time to waste, I munched down on my burger, enjoying the peace and serenity I was surrounded with.

I was just about to take the last bite of my burger when my alarm suddenly went off.

"Shit..." I cussed, looking around to see if anyone noticed, but fortunately, no one seemed to have heard it, and if they did, they didn't care enough to show it.

That alarm reminded me I needed to head back to Wolfgate, so I waved Nina goodbye before walking out of the Cafe.

The heaviness that hit me outside the double doors was like a blow on my face. I doubled my footsteps, putting as much distance between Smallie's and me before I changed my mind.

Walking down the paved path, I tried not to think about what awaited me at Wolfgate. The sight of the magnificent skyscraper alone was enough to make my heart beat fiercely against my ribs, leaving my palms sweaty with anxiety.

Biting down on my lips, I walked into Wolfsgate with all the courage I could muster. Relief flooded me when I realized that the doors were still unlocked, so I went in through the back door of the storage room like I always do.

I hadn't been to my desk all day, and I still needed to submit the daily report of the tasks assigned to me. To think that I wasn't even halfway through my punishment for the day made me want to pull my curls out.

The passion and commitment of Walter Wolfhard to making my life a living hell needs to be studied, but I can't even complain because he's my boss, and I need his money at the end of the month.

I pushed those thoughts to the back of my mind as I settled into work, hoping to make it through the rest of the day in one piece.

WALTER

I looked at my wall clock and was taken aback by the time that stared back at me.

How in the world was it 10 pm already?

I was sure the building was a ghost zone then, so I picked up my things in preparation to leave. I didn't want to think about the number of missed calls that awaited me. I had to turn my phone off because I needed ultra-focus to complete what I was working on before the end of the day.

My best friend Jonathan would always say, "Why don't you just delegate?"

As much as I want to delegate all my duties while cruising on a Yacht, I enjoy my job. No, I actually do, and I want to contribute to my company's growth beyond the system put in place for increased future development.

After a few minutes of arranging my stuff, I was ready to leave. Slipping my phone out of my pocket, I stared at the blank screen momentarily, wondering if I should turn it on.

I decided not to, slipping it back into my pocket before strolling briskly to the balcony. The view of the city from my office on the 30th floor was mesmerizing. Flickering lights of different colors glimmered like stars in the galaxy, starkly contrasting the darkness that blanketed the night.

Was this what it felt to be on top of the world? I wasn't so sure, but it was something close to this.

The serenity of the night was what I needed to bring my mind to rest. There was a lot I wanted to do, so much I wanted to achieve, but with so little time. At that moment it weighed down on my mind, but I just wanted to bask in the calmness surrounding me.

It was hard, of course, and I decided to give up halfway through. With a grunt of frustration, I walked back into my office. After checking if I'd forgotten any vital documents, I picked up my briefcase and left the office, heading home.

The hallways were deserted and a little haunted, especially with the piece of paper tossed about by the wind. A shuffling noise filled my ears as I was about to turn for the elevator, and I froze.

"Hello?" I called out, but I got no response. The noise continued; this time, it was a loud, thumping sound.

"Hello? Is anyone still in here?" I called out again, but the noise persisted. With the hairs at the back of my neck standing at attention, I followed the sound, which got louder and louder as I drew close.

It led me to the storage room, and I pressed my ears on the door. The shuffling sound of feet was loud and clear, followed by what sounded like books slamming on a shelf and a whimsical female voice.

Are ghost workers real? But it wasn't even midnight yet. Swallowing the fear that tried to cripple my thoughts, I pushed the door open to reveal whatever was on the other side.

As the door swung open, a loud shriek followed, which made me yell in shock.

"ARRGH!"

"ARGH!"

"Oh…" I paused, quickly regaining my composure, realizing it was just Hailey Hernandez.

Her face was pure horror; eyes bulged out with a baseball bat raised in the attack.

Where did she even get a bat from?

I stared at her quizzically as she lowered her weapon, removing something plugged into one of her ears.

I glanced at it momentarily, realizing that was where the whimsical music was coming from.

"Good evening Sir." Hailey greeted, her tired grey eyes staring ghostly at me.

"What in the world are you still doing here? Everyone else has gone home." I questioned, taking in the disheveled girl in front of me. Her ruffled curls, sunken eyes, and slouched posture made my stomach twist in discomfort.

Who am I kidding? I asked her to do this. I literally told her not to leave until she completed the task, or else she shouldn't return the next day.

She squinted in confusion, "Because you told me to? I had to finish this if I wanted to keep my job."

"Oh." I replied, nodding as she slapped the truth on my face. Guilt washed over me, and suddenly, none of this felt right.

I cleared my throat, my eyes running over what she had done. "It's… it's pretty late, Ms. Hernandez. You should go home." I said to her, turning my back to leave, but she didn't move an inch.

"Yes, Sir, I just need to complete—"

"I said leave whatever it is you're doing and go home. Now." I ordered, and she half-ran out of the room without looking back.

We arrived at the elevator simultaneously; Hailey entered: she shuffled awkwardly to the side as I got in after her.

As we went down to the ground floor, boring elevator music was the only thing filling up the deafening silence, I glanced at the girl a few feet from me, and discomfort was spelled over her features.

For her sake, I couldn't wait for the elevator ride to be over. It didn't even look like she was allowing herself to breathe with her chest heaved slightly and her jaws tightly clenched.

The elevator chimed, and Hailey dashed out before the doors even opened. I snickered, walking over to the parking lot. It was dark and haunting, just like the rest of Wolfgate at night. Without waiting to be visited by whatever lurked in the dark, I got into my car and drove out of the building.

Hailey was right at the corner of the street, trying to flag down a taxi. I slowed to a stop in front of her, winding down the window facing her.

"Hop in, Hailey."

"Um…I-Thank you, Sir, for the ride, but I don't think we're going the same way—"

"Hailey, I'm not going to leave you out here because it is my responsibility to ensure my staff is safe." I explained. "Now, get in Hailey."

Without another word, she stepped into the car, muttering an almost indecipherable 'thank you' as she sat.

"So…where are we taking you?" I asked, tapping on my steering wheel.

"Foxglove…Foxglove road, Sir." She answered.

"Alright then." I started the ignition, and we drove off into the night. It was a quiet ride, with Hailey sitting stiffly on the chair like it stung.

"Relax." I said.

"Huh?"

"Relax, Ms. Hernandez." I repeated.

"I'm not going to punish you for relaxing after work hours."

She nodded, her shoulders dropping in relief. I wondered what kind of boss I was if Hailey Hernandez was this terrified of me. Was it just her, or did everyone else see me this way?

We arrived at Foxglove a few minutes later, and Hailey turned to me with a quivering smile that lit up her face.

"Thank You, Sir." She said profusely, and she ran off without waiting for my response.

"What a strange girl." I thought to myself as I watched her run off into the night.

HAILEY

$\mathcal{I}$ wiped the tears which slid down my eyes as my bus drove past a hospital. With my cheek pressed against the glass, my teary eyes watched in longing. It's been days since I visited my mum at the hospital, and guilt consumed me whole, gnawing at my insides.

After that day, Mr. Wolfhard dropped me off from work; I knew I had to make some sacrifices if I didn't want to lose my job. Usually, I'd stop by the hospital to check on Mum before heading to work. However, journeying to the hospital and then to Wolfsgate affected my job, so I decided to extend my morning hospital visits to the weekend.

So far, I've gotten into fewer clashes with Management, which meant fewer punishments and more productive hours to get things done. As unique as that was, I couldn't fight the sinking feeling.

The bus hit a bump, and I held my head in pain as it collided with the window pane. That knocked me off my reverie and brought me back to the present.

I arrived at Wolfsgate, walking through the front door confidently because I was certain only a few persons would have arrived at that time.

"Good Morning Mrs. Hans." I greeted the receptionist, who smiled back at me.

"Oh, hi honey, how are you?"

"I'm feeling great; how are you?" I asked her, genuinely concerned.

"Ugh? I can't seem to get this old piece of junk working. Other than that, I'm great." Mrs. Hans explained.

I eyed the system warily.

"Can I take a look?"

"Of course, knock yourself out." Mrs. Hans stepped back, and I tinkered with the system for some minutes. It just needed minor reprogramming in a few minutes; I was done.

"There you go, Miss Hans." I said as the home screen came to life.

Relief flooded her face as Mrs. Hans looked up from her computer, her lips forming a warm smile.

"You're such a lifesaver, Hailey. Thank you so much!" She wrapped her arms around me in a warm embrace.

"You're welcome." I said with a smile, heading up to my office.

The day was going pretty well, except for the lingering guilt in the pit of my stomach for not stopping by the hospital to see Mum. I arrived at my office and got to work immediately. I needed to finish early, to leave work on time to visit my mum at the hospital.

The hours went by quickly, and a knock on my door drew me out of the paperwork I was drowning in.

A mass of brown waves poked in, followed by the familiar warm smile belonging to Mrs. Hans.

"Hi, sweetie; I hope I'm not distracting you from much work." She asked as she walked in with a paper bag.

"Oh, it's fine. I needed the break." Out came my response.

"Well, I just thought to bring you some lunch to say thank you for earlier." Mrs. Hans handed me the paper bag, and my face lightened up.

"Aw, you didn't have to…" I cooed as I felt the warm food in my hands. "Thank you so much, Mrs. Hans."

"I should be the one thanking you…for everything." Mrs. Hans replied before walking out of the office.

My smile remained intact long after she had gone, pulling out the warm lunch from the paper bag. It was a cup of warm latte, a burger, and chips, and my smile widened.

I munched down the food with gratitude, realizing I had worked into my lunch break. Mrs. Hans may not know it, but she was also a lifesaver.

I had barely digested my lunch when the annoying cry of the company telephone rang in my ears.

"Hailey Hernandez here." I answered, and Tanya's voice soon filled my ears.

"Mr. Wolfhard asks that you come to his office; Now."

My heart skipped a beat, but I tried to keep my cool.

"Alright. Thank you, Tanya." She grunted as a response right before ending the call.

My hands were growing sweaty, and my heart threatened to burst out of my chest as it rammed against my ribs.

What did he want now? I was at work early and even worked into my lunch break. Wasn't this what he wanted?

Dread washed over me as I lifted my eyes at the familiar oak door. There was no need to delay the inevitable, so I walked in.

Tanya barely acknowledged my presence, and I couldn't care less. I had to focus on what was ahead of me,

I landed a few knocks on the CEO's door, which opened. I had no idea how he could do that with his door, but that soon left my mind when I stood before Walter Wolfhard, his forest-green eyes watching me from underneath his lashes.

"Miss Hernandez…" Mr. Wolfhard called out, my name rolling out of his mouth in a way that made my stomach flutter. What in the world is wrong with me?

"Sir." I forced out, keeping my voice as firm as possible.

"Take a seat," He gestured at the chair at the other side of the table. I eyed it momentarily before taking my seat on the plush leather chair.

An awkward silence followed, with Mr. Wolfhard staring at me with his hand on his chin as if he was in deep thought. My mind raced as I tried to figure out what this was about.

I couldn't hold Mr. Wolfhard's eyes for over a few seconds. My eyes lingered everywhere else, but his was like a laser, focused on me. I felt like I was about to explode under his prying gaze when he finally spoke.

"I heard about what you did." He began, finally taking his eyes away from my face. Cold washed over me as his words landed. It made no sense because I did nothing wrong today.

"Mrs. Hans told me about how you fixed the company's system...am I right?" He paused, lifting his eyes to look at me.

"Yes, Sir," I replied, and a wave of relief flooded my chest.

"That's very good." He muttered, typing something on his desktop. "So you studied computers or what?"

"No, not really." I answered. "I've just tinkered with that thing long enough to know what's wrong most times."

"I see." He mumbled absentmindedly like he didn't hear a thing I said but needed to give a response. I just sat there, trying not to stare at him for too long.

His jet black hair was slicked back, definitely held in place by a truckload of gel. His jaw ticked as he squinted his bottomless eyes at the screen. I swallowed.

It was hard to believe that such a handsome man was a mean asshole, but then a person can't have everything, can they?

"I have a new assignment for you, Ms. Hernandez." He began, finally turning his attention back to me. The printer whizzed beside him, and with his eyes still locked on mine, he reached out for the paper and snatched it from the printer.

"I believe you can achieve these with me, Hailey Hernandez. You have potential." Mr. Wolfhard's full lips stretched into a tight smile as he handed me the paper.

I reluctantly reached out to take it, eyeing the paper warily. My eyes ran over the content, and they widened in horror.

"S-Sir…I don't know what you heard about me, but I don't want to disappoint you. These are…pretty big tasks and—"

"You did not seem to comprehend me." Mr. Wolfhard reclined in his chair, amusement dancing in his eyes.

"We are. Of course, I won't leave such an important project in the hands of a teenager."

Ouch. For some reason, that felt offensive even though it held an element of truth.

"Of course, you will be compensated for these extra tasks, but I need you to be level-headed and focused on them. Do you understand?"

Words couldn't find their way out of my throat, so I nodded.

"Hailey you have impressed me with your determination and technical skills, I didn't know I employed a Wizard." Mr Wolfhard deadpanned. "Or maybe a lizard, you don't seem to be convinced about this, and I don't need a half-hearted mind for this project."

I clenched my fist, holding back the snarky comment dancing at the tip of my tongue. It's funny how it took a jab at my personality to get words flowing from my lips again.

"I'm going to ask you again, Ms. Hernandez. Do you understand?" He leaned in, and I reflexively sunk back into my chair.

"Yes, Sir." I replied, stifling the whimper bubbling in my stomach.

"Good." He straightened,

"Now, go ahead and wrap up your task for the day so that we can begin as soon as possible."

His sentence made me realize that the possibility of me seeing my mum at the end of the day was slim, and I didn't know how to feel about that.

"Yes, Sir." I replied, rising to my feet and walking towards the door under Wolfhard's piercing gaze.

WALTER

"Hello, Sir, I just—"

"For Pete's sake, Tanya, don't you know how to knock?" I snapped, shooting her a hot gaze from where I was seated.

"I-I'm so sorry, Sir." She stuttered, shutting the door and knocking once again.

"What is it, Tanya?" I drawled, and she slowly cranked the door open.

"You...sent for me, Sir." She replied, confusion written over her face.

"No, Tanya, I asked you to send for Hailey Hernandez." I sighed in exasperation. "Are you hard of hearing?"

"I'm so sorry, Sir; I guess I was a little too...distracted." Tanya replied in a deep, sultry voice. That would have been pleasant if I wasn't trying to catch up on a lot of work. Now, she just sounded irritating and desperate; I wasn't about to be quiet about that.

"Tanya, you do know you can lose your job because of this…nonsense you're doing right?" I asked her, wearing a frown on my face.

Taken back by my question, she fumbled.

"I-Um-I'm sorry, Sir."

"Your lack of professionalism can put all your hard work to shame, so take this as a warning. Do you understand?"

"Yes, Sir." She stiffly nodded.

"Now send in Hailey Hernandez and tell her to be quick." I dismissed, returning my attention to my screen as Tanya's heels clicked away.

A few minutes later, another knock landed on my door, and I groaned in frustration.

It better not be Tanya because my patience was running thin.

"Come in." I sighed, leaning back on my ergonomic chair, which slowly rotated under my weight.

In walked Hailey, her frizzy blonde curls, which were let to roam wild and free earlier, were now pulled back with a hair tie, accentuating her angelic features. Her eyes were tired but still warm and unfocused, darting about like the waves of the sea on a sunny day.

Her nose stood small and pointy; light shimmered on her plump red lips, which distracted me more times than I could admit.

I had no idea I was staring at her so overtly until she cleared her throat.

"Um, you're right on time Ms. Hernandez." I stated,

"Come on, we have a lot of work to do."

Hailey took her seat, and we got down to business immediately. Halfway through my explanation, I noticed her eyes stray toward my window, distant and distracted.

"Hailey." I called out, and she snapped back in shock.

"Are…you okay?"

"Um, yes, of course, I'm sorry." She apologized, turning her attention back to what I was talking about.

"What were you saying?"

With narrowed eyes, I watched her before I asked the question lingering in my mind.

"Are you hungry?"

"I-I'm doing great, Sir; I'm sorry for being distracted." She quickly chipped in, staring at the documents on the table.

"Well, you didn't answer my question." I arched a brow. "Come on; let's get you something to eat."

"You don't have to—"

"I wasn't asking, Hailey Hernandez." I said to her, and that was enough to keep her quiet.

"A quick sandwich won't hurt, so get up on your feet now."

"The kitchen is this way." I led the way, knowing she would follow. Her tiny footsteps clicked behind me, and for some reason, it made me chuckle.

I walked over to the fridge and took out a loaf of bread, peanut butter, and avocado before returning to the counter, where Hailey stood awkwardly.

"So, how do you make your sandwich?" I asked her, and with a shy smile, she walked over to the sink to wash her hands before picking up the loaf of bread and slicing it thinly.

I picked up a second loaf, making my slices while glancing at her.

"Don't mind me, I'm just learning." I chipped in, and she chuckled.

She sliced off the crust at the corners, and I smiled.

"Someone knows how to make a good sandwich."

"I don't think anyone eats their sandwich with the crust on…" She snickered, putting some peanut butter on her bread.

"Tell that to my old friend Isaac." I replied. "He would tell you that the crust is the best part."

Hailey picked up a crust and dropped a part of it. She scrunched up her nose and shook her head.

"No way, your buddy needs his taste buds checked."

We burst into laughter, and hearing her laugh for the first time felt good. It was melodic and soothing, a sound I could never get tired of listening to.

Chapter 5

WALTER

$\mathcal{I}$ lay on my bed in darkness, letting my mind run wild before surrendering into the arms of sleep.

Falling asleep was never easy for me, caused by my endless sleepless nights many years ago when I started Wolfsgate.

A wistful smile crept on my lips at the memories of my early days with Wolfsgate. It took a lot of toil, sweat, and tears to get me where I was, and I knew I was yet to reach the apex of my potential.

It was a lonely journey, with only a few friends sticking by during tough times. Now I was surrounded by people, but no one ever got too close. I knew why they were here and could see through their genuine cackles of laughter and saccharine smiles.

Hailey's laughter filled my ears at that moment, and I smiled. Her giggles were so pure and warm, and her smile was like a lightbulb, making her eyes glisten with such intensity.

It was fascinating. She was fascinating.

I remembered the first day I saw her at Wolfsgate. I was headed for a board meeting, and she was walking with Simone Wang, the head of the Human Resources department.

My eyes trailed after her, and Tanya Genova, my assistant, seemed to notice my fascination.

"That's Hailey Hernandez." She scoffed.

"Can't believe Simone thought that little girl would be the best person to fill Reggie's shoes."

"You should learn to mind your business, Ms. Genova." I turned to Tanya, and she went silent the rest of the way.

I spared Hailey one last glance before walking into the boardroom. Later that day, I looked up her employee file, and that was when Tanya's words began to make sense.

Hailey Hernandez was just eighteen!

What in the world was Simone thinking? So far, he has successfully hired the best staff for Wolfsgate, but his recent selections made me doubt his expertise.

But Hailey's results proved me wrong, and it wasn't enjoyable to admit it. Her ideas always turned out excellent even though they were unique, and it caused a lot of rift between us.

A little wonder I always looked for the slightest opportunity to punish her.

"Ugh, what was I thinking?" I asked myself.

A frustrated groan escaped my lips as more embarrassing memories flooded my mind. Sleep didn't seem to be calling anytime soon, so I changed into my workout clothes and headed downstairs to the gym.

I couldn't stop thinking about Hailey and our time working on the new project together. I barely know her, but so far her positive qualities out way any negative ones by far, Hailey has already made an impact on my life. The fact that just the thought of her enabled me to breeze through a four hour workout and me not enough realize how quickly the time had passed. I take a quick glance at my watch after wiping the sweat from my forehead.

"Crap 6:30 AM!" I yell out throwing down my sweat soaked towel as I hurried to the upstairs shower.

While I get ready for work I got a burst of joy that passed through me. Dressed to impress I head off to Wolfgate. Excited, I will soon be in the company of the breath of sunshine, Hailey Hernandez.

HAILEY

I was seated in Mr Wolfhard's office, staring at him as he spoke, but my mind was far from present. I had gotten a call from the hospital that my mum was awake, and all I wanted to was see her, but I was stuck here with my boss.

"Hailey."

I pictured my mother's smile, her kind eyes looking up, and her calm voice calling out to me.

"Hailey."

I've missed her embrace. The way she wrapped her arms around me like she was protecting me from all the evils in the world made me feel safe and protected, and I just wanted to be with her—

"Hailey Hernandez!"

I jumped at the sound of my full name, staring right back at Wolfhard's face, mere inches away from mine, as he peered with concern.

"What in the world just happened to you?" He asked, waving his hand in front of my face. "Can you see me?"

"Yes, I can; I'm so sorry, I—"A tear slipped from my eyes, and I quickly caught it before Mr. Wolfhard noticed, but his eyes were keener than I thought.

"Are you…crying?" He lifted my chin to face him, and warmth spread over my stomach.

"No, I'm sorry—I'm….gosh so sorry Sir." I wiped my face furiously.

Mr. Wolfhard's hard exterior softened, and he poured me a glass of water.

"Here." He handed me the glass, and I muttered my thanks.

"I know it's way past closing time, and you're clearly not okay, so would you like me to drive you home?"

I shook my head from side to side, "N-no Sir, thank you."

"Hailey, look at me." He said, tilting my chin to face him. "I want you to talk to me or at least let me take you home…I can't leave you like this."

I fought hard, contemplating if I should tell him about my mum. Isn't he just going to find me pathetic? But then, he asked for it, and I don't even think I can drive alone in this state.

"Come on." He rose to his full height, beckoning me.

"Let's get you some fresh air; this office is suffocating."

I followed behind him, and we exited to his balcony overlooking the metropolis.

We took our seats on the handwoven chairs, soaking in the serenity of the night.

"Take your time… I'm ready to listen when you're ready." Mr. Wolfhard said, and I sighed.

"Mr. Wolfhard, I—"

"Walter." He interrupted. "For this moment, I'm your very good friend Walter who wants to listen to you...so talk to him."

The sincerity in his eyes reached deep into my soul, peeling off the layers of my mind bit by bit.

"It was a regular day, and I was hanging out with my friend, Stacy." I began, staring into the distance while letting the flickering lights distract me.

"Then I got a call from the hospital that my mum…was in an accident."

I sniffed, looking down at my reflection in the glass of water. "Seeing my mother in such a critical state was life-changing...I had to get a job, and here we are."

I glanced at Walter, and his glassy eyes caught me off-guard. Or it was a trick of the light; I wasn't sure.

"She's been in a coma for almost a month, and I just got a call before I came in here that she…she was awake." My voice betrayed me at this point, trembling as tears freely rolled down my face.

"Wow, that's uh… that's amazing." Walter replied,

"Why didn't you tell me?"

I blinked at him incredulously, "You're…my boss."

"Your point exactly?" Walter raised an eyebrow.

"I just…I didn't want you to think that I was looking for an excuse to leave. I know I've been getting in trouble a lot recently, so I was…trying to make up for it and be a good staff."

"That is ridiculous." Walter shook his head, "I know I'm your boss and all, but I'm human too."

"Are you? Or are you an Alien from Timbuktu?" I realized that was a lame joke a little too late, but Walter was already doubling over with laughter.

"Come on, let's get you to the hospital." Walter rose to his feet, extending his hand towards me. I reluctantly placed my hand in his, and we walked together to his car.

My eyes constantly darted to our interlocked hands, and warmth spread over my chest. Why was I even overthinking this? He's just a good boss, a friendly and kind human-like person like me who had a soul.

No wonder I felt strange about it.

I wasn't shocked to see a different car waiting in the parking lot; I didn't expect the CEO of Wolfsgate to have just one ride. All his vehicles always looked and smelt so new, like he was riding them for the first time, but I kept my ridiculous thoughts to myself as I sat in the car.

We rode into the night in silence, except for the radio, which croaked a popular pop song I caught myself humming.

"You listen to Gina?" Walter asked, and I bobbed my head.

"Not like I was given a choice. Her song is literally everywhere." I admitted.

"I mean, you're right, but do you listen to her by yourself? Do you even like Gina's songs, or does peer pressure influence you?" Walter asked, keeping his eyes on the road.

"Fine, fine, you caught me." I raised my hand in surrender. "I'd rather listen to The Blakes and Finleys. They're the most underrated band out there."

Walter slowly turned his head towards me, eyes gleaming with shock like he had just found a long-lost treasure.

"You know The Blakes and Finleys?" He asked in a surprisingly high-pitched voice.

"Well, yes. Weird, I know, but a girl loves what she loves." I shrugged.

"Hailey, I bought the entire front row of the last Blakes and Finleys concert. That's how much I love them."

I stared at him in disbelief. "No way....there is no way you have such a good taste in music."

Walter's smile slowly disappeared. "What do you mean by that? Of course, I do."

"Okay, I'm surprised you even listen to music at all." I confessed, earning a glare from Walter.

"Sorry, sorry." I snickered. "But then, you're always so busy, and I never thought you'd have the time to discover gems like the Blakes and Finleys. I'm impressed."

"You're impressed?" Walter snickered.

"You're the one who's listening to a millennial band when you should be dancing to Gina the pop star like the rest of your mates."

I couldn't hold back my laughter, doubling how his pitch increased when he said, 'Gina, the pop star.'

"Alright, you win!" I threw my hands in surrender again.

"And we're here." Walter announced as he drove through the gates of St. Louis Hospital.

My smile faded as I looked up at the building towering over us.

"Hey…" Walter called my attention. I lifted my fearful eyes at him, letting him see my vulnerability.

"I don't know what to expect in there." I admitted, gesturing towards the hospital cascading entrance doors. "And I feel terrible for not being there when she woke up."

"Don't beat yourself up over something you can't control, Hailey." Walter said. "And it's okay to not know how to react when you see your mum. Just be yourself."

I nodded at his words.

"Thank you, Sir. I'm really grateful for this."

"It's nothing, Hailey." He said with a tight smile. We both sat there, locked in each other's gaze, and I could tell myself getting lost in his forest green eyes. He stretched his hand towards my face, tucking a stray curl that slipped from my hair band.

His fingers grazed my cheeks, leaving a trail of warmth as he withdrew them. Did he feel what I felt, or was it all in my head?

His lips parted in a smile so warm and inviting that my lips tingled at the sight of his. I blinked back at the thoughts, clearing my throat.

"Would you…like to come with me?" I reluctantly asked.

"This is a special moment for you and your mum, Hailey. Maybe I'll say hello another time." Walter replied, and I nodded.

"Thank you…so much." I said with gratitude.

"You're welcome." He chuckled. "Go on now, Hailey Hernandez."

"Yeah…right." I flashed him a smile before stepping out from the car.

I could feel his eyes on me as I walked, and when I turned back, our eyes locked again. Ignoring the flutter in my chest, I walked through the hospital's double doors, headed for my mother's ward.

My legs trembled with every step, with fear and anticipation mingling in my mind. I was excited, but then apprehension nibbled away at my joy. Damning those thoughts, I doubled my steps.

I was going to see my mum's beautiful smile again.

My steps grew into a jog, and before I could stop myself, I had broken into a run.

"No running in the hospital!" One of the nurses yelled behind me, but no one stopped me. I let the fear and the excitement fuel me, and by the time I arrived at the front of her ward, I was a sweaty, panting mess.

Sucking in a sharp breath, I cracked the door open and trembled with horror, eyes wide as I stared at the person beside my mother.

"Hi, honey." Dad greeted, wearing a wrinkly smile on his face.

HAILEY

"Dad?" I muttered in disbelief, staring at the man seated beside my mother. I couldn't take my eyes off him, and my shock soon turned into anger.

"What is he doing here?" I asked the nurse attending to Mum, but Mum spoke before she could say anything.

"Honey…" Mum's feeble voice called out to me, and I ran to her side while keeping my eyes on my dad.

To think that this man who disappeared without a single goodbye was right here in the same room with me made my skin crawl.

However, I didn't come there for him. I came to see my mum, so I turned to her, tears brimming when she smiled at me.

"It's so good to have you back, Mum," I said, wrapping my arms around her. I couldn't hold back the tears, letting them run down my face while I basked in that precious moment with my mum. I'd almost forgotten that my father was still in the room until he spoke.

"I've really missed this."

I looked up to see him wiping his eyes, and my face contorted into a scowl.

"You do not have the right to use those words, Dad."

"Hailey—"

"No, let me finish." I rose to my full height, my eyes still locked on him. "So you disappear without a word or even a goodbye, and three years later, you waltz in here saying something about 'missing this'?"

"Hailey, please…" Mum's feeble voice pleaded with me, but I was too blinded in my rage to listen.

"Who told you you had the right to be here right now after everything you've done?"

He slumped in shame, and his eyes lowered to his intertwined fingers.

"You don't understand, Hailey."

"Of course, I don't understand." A humorless laugh escaped from my lips. "And I don't think I care to listen to your lies. Now leave."

"Hailey, don't say that…" Mum scolded me weakly. "That's your father you're talking to,"

"I don't think he deserves to be called that any longer." I remarked. "A father doesn't walk out on his own. A father doesn't abandon his family."

He rose to his feet, walking towards me, but I raised my hand to stop him.

"This was a special moment for me and my mum, but here you are, ruining everything." I gritted my teeth with every word. "What do you want from us?"

My resolve was wearing off, and I could already feel myself breaking.

Dad just stood there, staring at me with gleaming eyes.

"I know that no explanation will be enough to justify what I've done, but believe me when I say that I thought about you two every day."

"How do you expect me to believe that?" I asked him. "You could have called, texted, or something, but you didn't, and that told me all I needed to know."

He wiped his eyes with his shirtsleeves while I forced the sobs threatening to find their way to my mouth, down my throat.

"Hailey, don't do this…" Mum whimpered, and I took her hand to comfort her, but I wasn't about to let things go just like that.

He stared at me with tear-filled eyes, but I held his gaze, fiery and determined to keep to my word. He let out a defeated sigh before slowly walking out of the ward.

I turned to the nurse in anger. "How could you let a stranger in just because he claims to be my dad?"

"I'm really sorry, Ms. Hernandez, he brought proof, and we couldn't refuse him." The nurse apologized profusely.

"How did he even know about my mum and this hospital?" I asked the nurse, who looked like she had seen a ghost.

"I…asked to see him."

I turned sharply to see Mum struggling to sit up, and the nurse immediately ran to her side.

"What do you mean, mum?" I asked in confusion.

"When I woke up, I asked them to call you…and your father." She barely muttered.

"Why…?" I questioned. "Why, mum? I don't understand…"

"Do you know why your father left, Hailey?" Mum asked, and I shook my head from side to side.

"He was…." Mum wiped her eyes, her chest heaving with every breath.

"He was going to destroy himself if he didn't go…"

The nurse turned to me. "Your mum is really weak and needs some food, rest, and a lot of sleep. How about you guys talk about this when she feels better?"

"Okay…" I nodded, wrapping my arms around my mum.

"It's so good to have you back, mum… I've missed you."

"I've missed you too, honey, "Mum replied. "I'll see you soon."

I stepped out of the hospital, and there he was, seated on one of the benches. I stared at him momentarily, and all the family memories started rushing into my mind.

Beautiful memories that ripped me apart in pain.

I stormed towards him, wiping the tears in my eyes.

"Why are you still here?"

He lifted his tired eyes, and a small smile tilted his lips upwards.

"Hailey…"

"What do you really want, Dad?" I broke, unable to hold it in any longer. "To hurt us again?"

"Oh Hailey, I'm so sorry…" Dad pulled me into his arms, and I wept hard. I hated talking about him or thinking about him because the pain of him leaving wrecked me in many ways.

His gentle pats on my back reminded me of the days when he was indeed present, and it hurt so much.

"I miss you so much, Dad." I admitted, "Why did you ever leave?"

Dad sighed, his eyes staring straight ahead.

"I…I had to leave Hailey."

"The question is why, Dad. Why?" I was getting agitated, which was evident with every word I spoke.

"Because if I had stayed, it would have destroyed us all, Hailey." Dad's voice broke, and his eyes bore so much pain that I couldn't take to look at them for too long.

"I had to go to rehab and promised your mum I'd come back when I was at least six months clean. It's been a hard couple of years since I left."

Those words struck me like lightning, and I blinked in confusion.

My dad was an…addict? I turned to him, and he only smiled wearily at me.

"Take as much time as you need to process it, honey."

I bobbed my head absentmindedly, trying to connect the dots. I could have sworn my dad was great before he left, but now that I think about it, it was starting to make a lot more sense.

"I hope you can find a place in your heart to forgive me, Hailey." Dad sighed, rising to his feet. I watched him walk away, and as he disappeared down the hallway, the dam in my eyes was open, and I let the tears run freely down my face.

———

WALTER

"You have an email from Montgomery, Sir." Tanya stated as I walked into the office.

"Good morning to you too, Ms. Genova." I breathed, taking long steps toward the door of my office. I tried hard to hide it, but the anxiety courting through me at Tanya's news made my insides twist and turn.

With sweaty palms, I tapped away on my laptop, my fingers hovering over the button that could change everything.

For weeks, Hailey and I, alongside the rest of the team, worked hard on this project, and the moment was finally here.

The more I worried about it, the more reluctant I was to open it, so I just pressed down on the enter key without thinking. Delay would keep the results the same and even jeopardize them.

My eyes roamed over the screen as I read through it wide-eyed. It was unbelievable.

"Yes!" I screamed at the top of my lungs, pumping my fist in the air.

"Sir, are you okay?" Tanya burst into my office, full of concern.

"Tanya, we did it!" I took her by the hand, twirling the stunned lady around before I ran out of the room, searching for Hailey.

My staff looked at me with shock as I skipped down the hallway, but I was too excited to care.

"Good morning Sir Wolfhard." Some of them greeted,

"Good morning, beautiful people!" I chirped in response, and the horror in their eyes was a delight.

After what felt like forever, I finally arrived at the door of Ms. Hailey's office.

I knocked once, cranking the door open, and there she was, my beautiful, brilliant genius.

She sprung up to her feet the moment I walked in.

"Good morning Mr. Wolfhard." She greeted, "what a pleasant surprise—"

I wrapped my arms around her in an embrace, and she stood there, frozen in shock.

"We did it, Hailey. We did it!"

I took her hands and spun her in circles, excitement coursing through me. Hailey was too stunned to speak, and her eyes were close to popping from their sockets.

When I was calmer, we sat down, and I explained everything to her.

"Montgomery loved our pitch, and they're willing to sponsor the product's release, Hailey."

Her hand flew to her mouth as her eyes crinkled with joy.

"Oh my gosh, this is a dream come true!"

"Yes…it is." I agreed. "All our sleepless nights and hours of toiling were not in vain, Hailey."

"And that makes me so relieved." She sighed, and I chuckled.

"I don't think you have any idea what this means for Wolfgate." I explained.

"We need to celebrate this success, just the two of us."

I rose to my feet, rubbing my chin in deep thought.

"Of course, the entire team will celebrate, but we worked the hardest on this, you know."

Hailey nodded, watching me with curiosity.

"How about a weekend trip to Wales?" I turned to her in excitement, and she just shrugged.

"Whatever you say, Sir."

I smiled, walking over to her.

"I know I've stretched you thin so many times, maybe a little too much sometimes but look at you. You didn't break, and that is so impressive."

Her smile turned into a proud grin, and her pretty eyes gleamed joyfully.

"All thanks to my mum. She taught me how to stay strong." Hailey replied.

"Your mum raised a beautiful, strong, and smart girl." I confessed, reaching out to tuck a stray lock of hair behind her ear. She shivered slightly at my touch, and I could feel the atmosphere slowly shift.

Her eyes roamed my face, lingering a little longer on my lips. Her eyes drew me in, and her lips were even more inviting. The gap between our faces began to slowly close until all that was left was a mere centimeter.

Her eyes darkened with want as I cupped her face in my palms, but suddenly I dropped my hands like her skin was made of coal, taking several steps away from her.

"Don't forget we still need to finalize the plan for Firtree..." I said, and she nodded.

I walked out of that office with the hairs on my body standing at attention. Hailey and I were a nod away from kissing right there in her office.

"Shit." I cussed, running my fingers through my hair. That would have been a disaster waiting to happen. I knew what I felt; clearly, I wasn't the only one who felt the energy crackling in the air.

It wasn't the first time we had such tension, but the pull was never this strong. At that moment, nothing else seemed to exist but only Hailey.

"This is so messed up." I thought, running my hands over my face as I entered my office. I was so confused, and my emotions were running haywire for the first time in a long time.

This was a deadly path I was about to tread, and so many things could go wrong.

But is it worth it? Could Hailey be the one I've been searching for?

So many questions bombarded my mind, questions I didn't have the answers to.

How long are we going to run away from this?

Chapter 7

HAILEY

I bit down on my lower lip, tapping my feet restlessly while waiting for Walter to call. Earlier that day I woke up after the sun was out, grateful for the weekend. It was a sunny Saturday and I was still sprawled on my bed when my phone suddenly vibrated to life, my ringing tone blaring loudly through the speakers.

Without looking, I stretched out my hand towards my bed stand, trying to turn off my phone only to end up answering the phone call.

"Hello Ms. Hernandez." A familiar baritone reverberated through the room and my heart stopped.

I shot up from my bed, snatching the phone from where it laid on the bed stand.

"G-Good morning Mr. Wolfhard." I stuttered, trying to sound as alert as possible.

"Good morning Ms. Hernandez. I trust your weekend is going well." Asked Walter and I nodded, half-forgetting that he wasn't in the room with me. Met with silence, I cleared my throat in realization that I actually haven't used my words.

"Yes Sir, it…is? "

My response sounded more like a question than an answer, and I mentally screamed at how unsure I sounded. I prayed in my heart that he wouldn't ask me to come to the office. Weekends are the only days I got to rest and I wasn't about to trade it just because he's my boss.

"Well, Hailey Hernandez, your weekend is about to get better." Mr. Wolfhard said, and I could hear the smugness in his voice as he spoke. "Get dressed, I've got a surprise for you."

I blinked, taking my phone away from my ears and placing it back to be sure I heard him right.

"A surprise?" I repeated. "For me?"

"Yes, Hailey Hernandez." Walter chuckled. "I'll pick you up in an hour."

A full minute passed and there I sat on my bed, still trying to make sense of what just happened. His last words rang in my ears and they were enough to get me on my feet.

I dashed to my wardrobe, trying to find some decent outfits to choose from but most of my clothes were in the laundry basket. I barely had any time to do my laundry in weeks and my decision to procrastinate had come to bite me in the butt.

"Arghhh!" I screamed into the pile of clothes on my bed, wondering what to do. I had only thirty minutes left and I still wasn't sure of what to wear.

I didn't even know where he was taking me, so how would I know the right outfit to put on to match the occasion?

With time running out, I ended up grabbing a red jumpsuit with a heart necklace and a corset to give that simple yet classy look.

I got dressed in a jiffy, pairing the jumpsuit with one of my mum's necklaces will have to do, given the short notice and limited wardrope selection.

"Gosh, mum is so going to kill me if she finds out." I said to myself as I stared back at my reflection.

My hair hung in loose curls, with no time to straighten it; I touched up my face with light make up. With one last glance at my messy room, I sprinted up to the living room to wait for Walter's arrival.

At exactly eleven o'clock, a series of knocks landed on my door and my trembling legs urged me towards it. I cracked the door open and my breath hitched as I stared at the man in front of me.

His intoxicating smell was the first thing that dominated my senses, and I tried so hard not to shut my eyes and take a deep breath just to soak it all in.

There he stood, towering over me with a small smile lingering on his full, luscious lips. His 5'0 clock shadow was gone, accentuating his sharp jawline which twitched as he tried to stifle his smile. His jet black hair fell in soft waves, giving him a handsome, playful look.

I tried to look everywhere except at his forest green eyes which beckoned to me in the softest of whispers. For a full minute, not a single word was said to each other as we both let ourself go in the moment.

But then, it was starting to get awkward really quick, and Walter seemed to enjoy watching me squirm under his torturous gaze.

"Ahem…" I cleared my throat. "Do I…need to change my clothes?"

That sounded like a random question, but as I took in Walter's vintage short sleeved shirt with the first two buttons undone and a pair of cargo shorts, I felt like I must have overdressed for this occasion.

"Hello to you too, Hailey Hernandez." His lips spread apart, letting out a brief chuckle.

"And no, you don't have to. You look amazing."

I opened my mouth to form a response but I ended up looking like a gaping fish.

"So…you wanna come in for a moment?" I finally asked, after several seconds of fumbling over words.

"No thank you, I'm here to whisk you away but I guess I just got a bit… lost in the moment." His voice was softer when he mentioned the last words and his eyes held mine with a fervency that made my face heat up.

"Let's go?" He asked, hand outstretched towards me and I nodded, hesitantly placing my hand on his.

Waiting right outside was an SUV, not sure of the brand because I was a bit distracted and I'm not so good with cars anyways, but it was clearly different from the ones I'd seen him drive to the office.

Standing beside it was a chauffeur, who opened the door as Walter and I drew close.

"Thank you." I muttered to him as I stepped into the sleek, new ride. My nostrils were greeted with the sweet smell of new, mingled with a car diffuser that smelled like it could buy my entire outfit.

"Are you okay?" Walter asked me with genuine concern on his face.

"Yeah." I lied, but obviously he could see through my body language that I wasn't as relaxed as I would if I was hanging out with friends or family.

"You couldn't lie to save your life, Hailey." Walter shakes his head. "Look, I understand how weird it is hanging out with the same boss who's probably a pain in your ass—"

I snorted, slapping my hand over my mouth with my eyes wide. Walter deadpanned, trying to stifle his laughter.

"—but today I don't want you to let that restriction hold you back from enjoying yourself. That's the essence of this in the first place. If you don't have fun, than it was all a waste so I want you to be yourself and be free okay? I promise I won't use it against you at the office. Do you understand?"

"Yes Sir." I bobbed my head.

"Walter, Hailey. My name is Walter, I've told you this before." He drawled.

"Right. Walter. Got it." I nodded and he chuckled.

"Gosh, you are something."

The rest of the ride was somewhat silent, except for the jazz music coming from the radio. I kept my eyes on the unfamiliar road we plyed, taking in the suburban areas and longing for the simplicity they enjoyed.

Life in the city was a hell of a ride, and it felt good to take a break. I still had no idea where we were headed, and I was too cautious to ask. He did say it was a surprise, but it wouldn't hurt to ask would it?

"We've been on the road for quite a while now." I hinted, watching for Walter's response from the corner of my eyes.

He lifted his eyes from his phone and turned to me.

"A surprise, remember?"

"Right." I huffed and he laughed.

"Don't worry, you'll love it." He assured me and for some reason that was enough for me.

The car began to slow down as we drove up a hill.

Ahead of us sat a cabin, with huge glass windows giving a clear view of the vintage interior. Unlike the regular cabin, this one was made with a modern voice that I couldn't wait to explore.

The car drew to a stop and I turned to him for confirmation that this was where we needed to be.

"We are here." Walter announced with a warm smile.

The cabin itself was just one of the wonders. As we stepped out of the car, I felt like I was being wrapped in the arms of nature.

"What is this place?" I gasped, taking in the wonderland that surrounded me. The grass underneath my feet was green and soft, with flowers growing on the west side of the hill. Somewhere in the distance was a spring, and the cheerful chirping of birds as they hopped from tree to tree aroused my inner child.

In that moment, all I wanted to do was to break into a run and let the wind carry me wherever it wanted.

"This, is the Wolf's paradise." Wolfhard answered, pride oozing from his voice.

"Come on, there's more you need to see." Wolfhard beckoned me, and I fell into step beside him. The interior of the house was as majestic as I imagined, with a vast living room area covered with spotless oaken floors and vintage furniture arranged in the most sophisticated way.

"I'm sure you're thinking, 'Why the hell did Walter bring me here?' " Walter mentioned, amusement dancing in his eyes.

I reluctantly nodded, taking a seat on one of the chairs in the living room.

"Well, we've had a stressful couple of weeks, and after the victory I thought about a creative way for us to celebrate. We could have easily gone to a hotel and have a nice meal but I wanted something that would be worthwhile and memorable."

He walked towards the other side of the room, pulling a chest from a corner. I watched him drag the chest to the center of the room, maintaining eye contact as he cracked the chest open.

"What do you think of a two person Blakes and Finleys' karaoke concert with your favorite meal and a rooftop dinner afterwards?" Walter pulled out several Blakes and Finleys' albums and I gasped, tears of excitement following my eyes.

"Yes...yes I'm in!" I squealed and Walter burst into laughter.

"Well then, let's get the party started!"

Walter turned on the music and in no time, my favorite song was blasting through giant speakers. He handed me a microphone while he held on to the other one, and I reluctantly retrieved it from his hands.

"Forget about what they say…" Walter began, his voice deep and soothing.

"In you I've found my own home…"His eyes beckoned to me as he sang, and I lifted up my quivering hands which clung tightly to the microphone.

"I've searched around, craved for me…" I sang, starting to get into the flow.

"But you were right here, the one I wanted!" we harmonized, and together we sang out hearts out as the chorus dropped, jumping around the large room like little kids.

"She said it was over, and deep down we knew that our love had barely begun!"

We screamed the outro of our fifth song, panting like we just had ran a marathon.

"That was electrifying…" I breathed, plopping down on one of the couches arranged around a gorgeous wooden coffee table.

"I haven't done this in forever…" Walter confessed, turning to me. "Hungry?"

I nodded and I squealed as he pulled me to my feet. I wrapped my hands around him in shock. Our faces were mere centimeters apart and our breaths mingled together.

"I'll…get the…steak…ready." He whispered, his eyes lingering to my lips before locking eyes with mine.

"Um…yeah…" I replied, but none of us moved from the spot, distance between us slowly closing. Heat rushed through my body, as his hand slowly slid up my back.

"What a time to be alive!" Gwen Finley's shrill soprano blasted through the speakers and we jumped apart.

Apparently, I had stepped on the remote, which pressed the play button.

How timely and…convenient.

While I was still recovering from that intense moment, Walter was already halfway across the room, walking briskly to the kitchen like nothing just happened.

I followed him behind, keeping my distance and he smiled when he turned around and saw me right behind him.

"So how do you like your steak?" He asked me, tying an apron around his waist. Whoever said men in a suit were hot haven't seen a man struggling to tie his own apron.

"Uh…a little help?" He asked and I couldn't hold back my laughter.

"I think you're tying the wrong apron, Walter." I pointed out, handing him over the bigger one while removing the smaller one from him. My heart rocked in my chest, slamming against my ribcage at how close we were once again and Walter's soft gaze on me wasn't helping.

"Why are you looking at me like that?" I finally found my voice, asking question that has plagued my mind all day.

"I like looking at you." He replied, his palms cupping my face. A shiver coursed through me as his hands touched my face, hypnotized by the intensity of his gaze.

He stared at me with longing, like he was struggling inside, at war with his emotions. Slowly, I lifted my hand to his face, lightly grazing his cheeks with my knuckles and he sucked in a sharp breath.

"Fuck this." He cussed, closing the distance between us as his lips touched mine. My eyes flung shut as I savored the moment, his soft lips sending jolts of electricity through my entire being.

For that moment I let myself forget that he was my boss, until it finally clicked.

I was kissing Mr. Wolfhard.

I tore away from him, shivering in fear.

"I'm…I'm so sorry I—"

"It's okay, Hailey. Don't apologize." Walter pleaded, pulling me close to him with his arms wrapped around my waist.

"When I'm around you, it's hard to focus on anything else, Hailey." Walter's husky voice whispered in my ears.

My knees almost buckled as his lips grazed the nape of my neck, sending a rush of warmth through me. In my muddled state I whimpered, grabbing a fistful of his hair and Walter let out a low growl.

"Hailey, What are you doing to me?"

"What… you've always wanted to do." I whispered, grabbing his face before pressing my lips against his.

Chapter 8

WALTER

My heart skipped a beat as I watched Hailey fall asleep on my shoulder as we rode back to the city the next day. The last 24 hours was surreal, but just like every other beautiful experience, it came to an end.

I tucked a stray hair falling from her bun and sighed. It felt good letting go of the reins with which I held my feelings bound, and even better knowing that she felt the same way.

Nothing was ever going to be the same again, but I didn't want to rush things. Hailey still had a lot to do and achieve, so for now I just wanted to support her journey and bask in what we have.

She stirred softly, nuzzling closer to my neck and I chuckled. How did she go from being my annoying employee to the girl who has invaded every inch of my mind. No matter how hard I tried to trace where it all started, I just couldn't place my finger on it.

She looked so peaceful as she slept, and my heart ached as I watched her. I wanted her so much that it hurt, I didn't want to ever let her go now that I've found her.

The beautiful memories we made at the Wolf's Paradise left a wistful smile on my face as I got lost in them. I was nudged back to reality when the car slowed to a stop in front of Hailey's apartment.

I didn't want to disrupt her beauty sleep, so I gently lifted her into my arms, while Thomas, my chauffeur, carried her bag.

"Open the door." I ordered Thomas who pulled out a bunch of keys from her bag. He was just about to insert the key to unlock the door when it flung open.

We were met with a man standing at the doorway, his eyes moving from Hailey who was still sleeping soundly in my arms to Thomas who was now a few steps away from the door.

"What's going on? What happened to Hailey? Who are you?"

The older man bombarded us with so many questions and I wasn't sure which to answer first. Hailey didn't speak much about her dad so I assumed he wasn't in the picture. If that was true, then who was the man standing in front of me and why was he in her apartment?

"Who are you?" I asked, holding Hailey closer to myself as he tried to take her from me.

"What the hell do you mean by that?" The man snapped. "I'm her father!"

"Hailey doesn't speak much about her dad, so I had to be sure." I replied, still keeping an eye out for his body language.

"Doesn't matter." He frowned, weighing me with his eyes.

"I asked a simple question… who's talking?" He asked again, getting agitated.

"Good day Sir. I'm Walter Wolfhard, Hailey's…friend." I forced a smile, even though all I wanted to do was to shove him aside and put Hailey to sleep.

I wanted to introduce myself as her boss, and it was right at the tip of my tongue until I changed my mind last minute. I didn't want to complicate matters any further. I was already sick of the questions.

"What happened to her? Is she alright?" He questioned further and I nodded.

"She's just sleeping…we had a work event yesterday and I'm sure she's just exhausted." I explained and he instantly relaxed.

He finally let me in, and I took her to her room. As I placed her on the bed, she wrapped her arms around my neck.

"Don't…go…."

"I have to sweetheart…I'll see you at work on Monday." I whispered; planting a brief kiss on her lips.

As I walked out of the house, I spotted a woman in the kitchen and a brief smile crossed my lips. I didn't need anyone to tell me who she was, I knew that was Hailey's mum at just one glance.

She didn't see me, so I didn't go over to introduce myself. Hopefully I'd get a better chance to do that.

Hailey's father gave me a long, hard look as I walked away, but I couldn't be bothered.

He couldn't do any damage.

My ride home was quiet, almost solemn and I couldn't shake away the emptiness that washed over me with Hailey gone.

I was never one to get easily attached to a woman, but if you found a rare gem, wouldn't you cling to it with your dear life?

HAILEY

I opened my eyes, looking around to be sure I was seeing right. I was in my house, and I had no idea how I got there.

The last thing I remembered was me sitting in the car with Walter so this could only mean that Walter was who got me to my bed himself.

Even though my room was a mess, his gesture still warmed my heart and the thought of him carrying me in his arms made my stomach flutter.

Several knocks landed on my door, putting a halt to my thoughts.

"Hailey?"

I sprang off my bed, bolting to the door, confirming I'd heard right.

I couldn't believe my eyes as I stood face-to- face with my mum who was grinning from ear to ear.

"Mum…mum!" I wrapped my arms around her, tears rolling freely down my face.

"I've missed you too, honey." She cooed, giving me a gentle squeeze.

"How did you get here? Why didn't you wait for me to come pick you up? I had no idea you would be discharged so soon." I blabbed, still trying to comprehend how my mum who was in a coma a week ago was standing in front of me.

"Your…father came." Mum replied. My smile faded so fast and I could see the disappointment in her eyes.

"Honey, he's working on himself."

"I know that, but I'm still trying to bring myself to accept the truth you know…for so long I'd convinced my mind to believe that he didn't want us anymore." I explained.

"I understand you, honey. Take your time, okay? I don't want to rush you or anything. "Mum's words were soothing and I couldn't help the tears that flowed from my eyes. She had no idea how much I've missed her presence, her food, her wise counsel, everything about her.

HAILEY

I had barely dropped my bags after a long day of work when my phone chimed.

I picked it up, a smile forming on my lips when I saw a message from Walter.

I miss you so much, ugh why did you have to go home?

My fingers danced on my screen as I typed a reply, sending it while biting down on my bottom lip.

All you could have done was ask me to stay:)

The next second my phone chimed again.

For real? Wait, don't tell me you're kidding.

I stifled the laughter bubbling in my stomach, lowering myself to my bed as I replied.

Fine, you got me. Just kidding!

His message came in a few seconds later.

Hailey Corey Hernandez! Don't play with my emotions like that!

I gasped, typing furiously in response.

Damn, you didn't have to bring my middle name into this.

Alright, you can have my last name, how's that for a fair trade? He replied.

I blushed so hard that my cheeks began to ache.

You're so corny.

I sprawled on my bed, staring at the rotating ceiling fan as I let my mind run wild.

You bring out the worst in me, lol

His response made me snort out loud, but he wasn't even done yet.

I just can't wait to see you on Saturday.

My stomach churned while my fingers ran over my screen. Earlier in the day, Walter told me about a charity event his mother was hosting and he pleaded that I come with him or else he would die of boredom.

I can't wait to see you too.

After sending the message, I sat upright again. Saturday was just in two days. What was I going to wear? Hell, I didn't even know basic rich people etiquette.

"Ugh, I'm so screwed!" I cried out, right before my mum yelled my name.

"Honey, dinner is ready!" mum's voice echoed.

"Coming!" I yelled at the top of my lungs, falling back on my bed afterwards as I reminised about the day at work. It was so exhausting trying to detach my emotions while working with Walter, especially when other members of staff were present.

Earlier in the day, Tanya almost walked in on us kissing and the way Walter barked at her in anger made me shiver.

"I'm sorry about that." Walter muttered, planting a kiss on the nape of my neck.

"M-maybe I should just… go…" I struggled to words out as his soft kisses distracted me.

"What if she comes back?"

"No. You don't have to." Walter replied, pressing me against his chest. "She wouldn't."

When I stepped out of Walter's office a few minutes later, Tanya's flaming eyes seared into my skin as I walked back to my office.

The thought of being hated more than I already was made bile rise up my throat, and I sat up in the bed. I decided to talk to Walter about it hopefully soon.

My stomach growled in hunger snapping me back to reality..

I quickly showered and joined my mum and dad for dinner. Dad has been coming around more frequently and I found myself starting to warm up to him.

"Hi sweetie, how are you?"

"Good evening Dad." I replied, taking a seat beside mum. I opened the sizzling pot and the aroma spread all around the room.

"Mhmmm, casserole." I grabbed a spoon, dishing hungrily.

"SOS, we've got a hungry lion on the loose." Dad exclaimed and we all burst into laughter. My phone chimed and I dropped it on the table, with the screen facing downwards.

"So how was work today?" Mum asked me and I shrugged.

"Just like every other day. Stressful."

My phone chimed again and I glanced it, before resuming my meal.

"So nothing interesting happened today?" Dad asked. At that moment, the memory of Walter's lips glued to mine before Tanya walked in flashed on my mind, but of course there was no way I'd tell my dad about that. Not even if there was a gun pointed to my head.

"Just work stuff mostly. We are working on a project that has been taking up a lot of time but at least we're making progress." I slurped a spoonful of soup, eyeing my phone which had once again chimed.

I picked it up, smiling at Walter's message.

Hello? Is anyone home? Gosh, where did you go?

"Hailey, no phones at the table remember?" Mum mentioned and my fingers froze over the screen.

"Just a minute mum." I pleaded, a smile lingering on my face.

"I don't know if you can see this Martha, but someone's got our daughter smiling like she just hit a jackpot." Dad pointed out with a knowing look on his face.

My face heated up and I looked away.

"Dad, stop!"

"Look at her cheeks, honey she's got someone." Dad was so excited, and it made me even more embarrassed.

"And she's not denying any of your claims, Mark…" Mum said to dad who just wiggled his brows at me.

"Young lady, so I get into and accident and I come back to find out you have a boyfriend?"

"Come on mum, don't say it that way." I hid my face behind my hands.

"But that's exactly what it is." Dad chipped in and I groaned.

"Dad, you're not helping!" I whined. turning to mum.

"Walter and I are—"

"Walter?" Dad asked, his face scrunched up in confusion.

"Uh…do you know him dad?" I asked, curious.

"The name rings a bell…" Dad scratched his greying hair, until his eyes lit up like a light bulb.

"The guy who brought you home from the work event?"

"Uh…yeah?" I replied, watching my dad with suspicion. I had no idea Walter met my dad, and he didn't mention anything about it so I didn't know where this was going.

Dad's face contorted into a frown,

"Are you serious, Hailey?"

"I... don't understand." An awkward laughter escaped from my lips.

"Isn't he like, twice your age?" Dad asked and I shrugged. "I don't know, maybe…but why does it matter?"

Mum and Dad exchanged a look, turning towards me at the same time with a solemn expression on their faces.

"Hailey, listen to me." Dad began, his voice trembling slightly. "We…we know how these things work, Hailey. That guy? He doesn't love you okay?"

"You don't know that." I replied defiantly. "You don't know him, Dad."

"You're right Hailey. I don't know him, but I know the likes of him and he is up to no good." Dad insisted and my tongue turned sour.

"What do you mean by 'the likes of him'?" I questioned. "You just see him once and judge him because he's older?"

Mum sighed.

"Hailey, you have to trust us." She glanced at dad for a moment, as if asking for permission to say something.

"We fear that he…that he's a groomer." Mum dropped the bomb and I rose to my feet.

"I love you, mum…but I won't let you disrespect Walter like that."

"We're not saying he is, we just recognise the patterns." Mum tried to explain.

Tears of anger spilled from my eyes and I shook my head.

"I can't believe you guys…"

"You don't have to Hailey, but maybe a little trust would not be so bad." Dad said, making my blood boil.

"And who are you to give sound judgement?" I snapped. "You walk out of my life without a word and you think you can just waltz back in and start dishing out unsolicited advice?"

"Hailey!" Mum scolded, but I was to furious to care.

My words seemed to have hit a nerve, because Dad's face fell.

"I never said I was a perfect Dad." He stated quietly. "But I will not sit back and watch my baby get hurt. Not when I can do something to stop it."

"I think that's my choice to make Dad, not yours." I replied, storming out of the room despite my parents please.

The door slammed shut after me and I slumped on my bed, letting hot tears roll down my face.

WALTER

I hated parties, these kinds of parties in particular but mum still insists on having me attend because;

"I might just find the woman of my dreams."

More like the woman of my nightmare.

Wasn't that where I met my ex, Eleanor? My jaw twitched at the thought of her being there. But do you know who else is going to be there? Hailey Hernandez. That was enough to put a smile on my face.

I stood in front of my full-length mirror, slicking a stray strands of my hair with my palms before leaving. Thomas had already brought my blue Tesla to the front, so I made myself comfortable.

"Foxglove road." I said to Thomas and he nodded, and the engines hummed to life as we hit the road.

My finger strayed to my pocket and I pulled out my phone, dialing Hailey's number.

I could have texted, but I just wanted to hear her voice. Gosh, you have no idea how much I've missed her. I waited anxiously for her to pick up, but as the call clicked to an end, disappointment washed over me.

A click away from calling her again, I decided against it. She was probably busy getting ready for the event so Id just have to be patient till I set my eyes on her in person.

After a few minutes, my phone vibrated. It was a message from Hailey and I was already grinning from ear to ear before I opened it.

She apologized for not taking my calls, explaining that she wasn't in the room when it rang.

I let her know it's fine, telling her we were close to her house. After sending her the message, I tossed my phone on the seat beside me where a bouquet of flowers laid.

The ride was a long one because of the growing traffic downtown, but after a short while we were parked in front of Hailey's apartment building.

I grabbed the bouquet of flowers I had gotten for her and walked up to her front door, landing a few knocks on the door.

The door cracked open and I swallowed hard, soaking in all of her beauty with my eyes. There she stood, in a stunning blue dress which matched her eyes. Her hair was curled in ringlets, with a few strands falling down the side of her face.

"Hello Mr. Wolfhard." She curtesied, her red lips parted into a smile that melted my heart into goo.

Wordless and breathless, all I could say was "Wow."

I handed her the bouquet and she looked at them like they were the most precious, fragile thing she's ever owned.

"You got me flowers? Aw, thank you so much." She whimpered, wiping at her teary eyes.

"I'd do anything for you. Hailey Hernandez." I meant every word that I spoke, planting a kiss on her forehead.

We were off a few minutes later, headed for mum's fifth annual charity ball of the year. Hailey squirmed in her seat, looking uneasy.

"What's wrong, Hailey?" I asked her.

"Wrong? There's nothing wrong. "She replied and I frowned.

"Yup such a bad liar, Hailey." I told her point blank. "Now tell me…what is going on?"

"You won't understand." Hailey replied quietly.

"Try me." I said, turning to give her my full attention.

"Come on, I'm listening."

Hailey stared into space, answering my question a few minutes later.

"I just don't feel like I belong." Hailey confessed. "What if I don't fit in? What if your mum hates me?"

"Woah, easy there sugar." I chuckled, "Where in the world are these thoughts coming from?"

"I dunno…you're in a different class than I am. What if your mum—"

I pressed my lips against hers, silencing her raging thoughts.

"You will be fine, Hailey. I promise."

We arrived at the party and Hailey's grip on my forearm tightened. I introduced her to a few friends and business moguls, keeping an eye out for mum.

"Walter?"

I turned around and she was right there, the woman I was looking for.

"Hello mother." I greeted, wrapping my arms around her in a hug.

"Good evening ma'am."

That was Hailey's voice cutting through the soft music that filled the room.

Mum's face lightened up like a child's, turning her attention to Hailey.

"Who is this gorgeous lady?" Mum walked over to Hailey.

"I'm Hailey Hernandez, Walter's—"

"Girlfriend." I completed, snaking my hand around her waist.

Mum took Hailey's hand in hers and patted it.

"You're such a stunning queen, Hailey Hernandez. "

"Thanks ma'am." Hailey replied.

"Oh, just call me Mrs. W. "Mum waved her hand dismissively, right before taking Hailey and walking with her as they talked.

"Well that was easier than I thought." I chuckled to myself, watching them with a smile on my face.

HAILEY

I massaged my aching temple, trying to keep my attention on the presenter. I had told Walter I had no interest in long, boring meetings that could have been an email, but he insisted I come along with him because I was a major part of the project.

A feathery touch grazed my thighs and I shot Walter a look. The man wore a poker face, eyes fixed on the speaker like he wasn't turning my legs into jello with his touch.

Like a statue I sat frozen, scared that any action would arouse suspicion or draw attention to us. I could barely hear a thing as my skin hummed long after Walter withdrew his hand.

"So, any questions?" The bald man asked and Walter raised his hand. My jaw almost hit the floor because how was he able to pay attention and distract me at the same time?

Walter asked him a couple of questions, while I watched on, dumbfounded.

Walter stayed back after the meeting, speaking with the CEO while I had to sit at the reception with Tanya.

Chewing loudly on her gum, she didn't hide the fact that she was staring at me.

I squirmed on my seat, keeping my eyes glued to my phone even though I was just hopping from app to app. It was the easiest way for me to distract myself from her piercing gaze but she didn't even flinch.

"How did you do it?"

I turned to Tanya, taking in her scrutinous gaze for the first time.

"How?" She repeated. "How did you do it, Hailey?"

I scrunched up my face in confusion, trying to make sense of her cryptic question.

"I have no idea what you're talking about…" I said.

"You see, that's the thing with you." Tanya rolled her eyes. "You know no one else is buying your feigned innocence right?"

"Cut to the chase, Tanya." My eyebrows furrowed in a frown. "What do you want?"

"Now that's more like it…" She snickered, straightening up. "I want to know how you got Mr. Wolfhard wrapped around your tiny little fingers, Hailey."

I couldn't hold back my laughter, wondering how long and hard she had thought about this before asking me.

"Are you kidding me right now?" I asked,

"I thought you were about to ask something groundbreaking, like how I was able to sit through that 4-hour long meeting without batting an eyelid."

Tanya scoffed. "I don't give a shit about that."

I leaned forward, running my eyes over her silky straight bob to her brown moccasins.

"This attitude is exactly why I have him wrapped around my fingers, and not you." I said with a sly grin. The double doors of the meeting room flung open at the perfect moment and in walked the man of the day.

Walter Wolfhard.

"All done, let's go." He beckoned us while he led the way.

"Hailey?" He called, hand stretched out to hold mine. I gave Tanya a wink as I placed my hand in his, walking side by side with Walter.

"So, how did it go?" I asked him.

"He said he just needs to put a few elements in place before we finalize Alistar, I'll be monitoring the progress on my end to ensure it all works out according to plan."

"I know it will." I reassured him just as we arrived at the parking lot.

"Is there anything else you need, Sir?" Tanya asked Walter.

"No thank you, that will be all." He replied before stepping into his car.

Tanya's eyes bore into mine with a menacing look, then she turned around and walked away.

I watched her disappear from sight, letting out a derisive snort before joining Walter in the car.

"What was that all about?" He asked me.

"I've never been Tanya's favorite person here, and she never ceases to remind me."

"Well baby girl, she lacks good taste." Walter said, planting a brief kiss on my lips. He turned on the car afterwards, driving out of Wolfgate into the unknown.

WALTER

The Blakes and Finleys blasted through the speakers as we road down the streets of Chicago. Hailey sang at the top of her lungs, not caring about the weird stares she got from other drivers at the red stop.

I bobbed my head along, trying to keep my eyes on the road while I rehearsed what I'd planned out in my head.

Hailey had no idea where we were going, which made it even better. She didn't seem to care either, and it warmed my heart to know she trusted me enough to keep her safe.

The sky was a pastel of orange and blue as the sun cast its warm golden glow for the last time before nightfall. We sat in silence, enjoying the serenity that surrounds us.

I'd caught Hailey staring at me for the third time, and I chuckled.

"Why are you stealing glances at me like I won't notice?"

"You weren't supposed to…" She chuckled, hiding her face behind her hands.

"Well I did, now explain yourself." I replied. Hailey only looked out the window, watching the trees racing past us as we sped into the distance.

"Hailey, are you okay?" I asked, concerned about the switch in her mood.

"Yeah, I'm fine I'm just…thinking…" Hailey replied, leaning on the window with her eyes strayed on me.

"A penny for your thoughts?" I asked, slowing down as we drew closer to our destination. It was a hilly road, somewhat deserted but the view was breathtaking.

"It's just…my parents." Hailey forced out the last words.

"And what about them?" I replied, pulling the car to a stop.

"Why didn't you tell me you've met my dad?" Hailey asked me.

"Well, I didn't think it was that important since we didn't exchange more than a few sentences." I shrugged, sinking further into the car seat.

"Did something happen?"

"Let's just say you're not my dad's favorite person at the moment."

"You don't say…" I said with a sarcastic smirk.

"I could have sworn I was on my best behavior."

"Walter…" Hailey said with a warning tone and I couldn't help but chuckle at her attempt to be strict.

She's just too adorable for that.

"It's not about your behavior, it's…he just doesn't trust you."

"Do you trust me?" I asked Hailey.

Her eyes squinted in deep thought for a moment, then she turned to look at me.

"I let you bring me to the middle of nowhere so yeah…I trust you, Walter."

"Then that's all that matters, Hailey." I replied, grazing her cheeks softly with my knuckles.

"Look, who cares if I'm your dad's favorite person? I'm his daughter's favorite and that's what really matters."

Hailey laughed, giving me a playful punch; which hit like paper but I groaned.

"Ouch, what was that for?" I pouted, rubbing the spot she punched.

"Nothing, just felt like it." She shrugged, looking out the window.

"So what is this place?"

When Hailey asked that question, I looked upwards, realizing we were missing the best part of the sunset.

I Jumped down from the car, jogging to the other side to open the door.

"Come on, Hailey, you don't want to miss this." I called out after her while running to the trunk to set up for the night.

"Okay, okay!" She snickered, coming down after me while trying to catch up with my pace.

I got so carried away while talking to Hailey that I almost forgot why I brought us out here. You can't blame me though, it's hard to not get carried away by Hailey's presence. But then, I had a whole night planned out so I knew I had to put in the work.

I kept the trunk open wide, pulling out the baskets from inside. The bigger basket contained clean sheets, blankets and pillows, while the smaller one bore some snacks and finger foods with wine and water.

"What are you doing?" Hailey questioned, taking in the chaos in front of her.

I climbed into the car through the trunk, detaching the backseats to create more space. After arranging the blankets and pillows to form a cozy bed, I unloaded the snacks and we both made ourselves comfortable.

The sun had gone down, and the cities down the hill began to light up almost at once.

"This..is...wow." Hailey watched wide-eyed, completely mesmerized by the view in front of us. She had no idea she was my best view.

"How did you even think of this? How did you discover this place?" Hailey asked me, genuinely curious.

"They say where a man's heart is, there lies his treasure." I replied, tucking some curls behind her ear.

Hailey's eyes gleamed under the starlight, listening to every word I spoke.

"I think about you all the time…" I confessed.

"I'm constantly thinking of the next thing to do to put a smile on your face."

Hailey's eyes moistened as her lips spread into a smile.

"You're too good to be true, Walter."

Her statement took me off guard, and I was too stunned to speak.

"Sometimes it's hard to believe that you're even real."

She continued, her hand slowly reaching out to touch me, to feel me.

"But you are…and you're always on the look out for ways to make me happy, I…feel like what I've done for you is a mere drop in the ocean, compared to what you have done for me."

Hailey's words warmed my heart, but I also found them amusing. How could she say all this when her existence alone is enough to make me happy?

"Stop laughing, I'm serious…" Hailey frowned and I pulled her closer to myself.

"I know you are, baby girl…" I planted a kiss on her forehead. "I find it amusing that you're trying to out do me."

"Well, a girl could try…" She mumbled, nuzzling closer to me.

"If only you knew your existence alone was enough…" I whispered, tilting her chin upwards to look into her eyes.

"You don't have to do anything to prove anything. Just having you by my side is enough. That's how much I love you, Hailey Hernandez."

Her eyes sparkled with tears, like the moon blessing the sea with its glow. Her eyes remained locked on mine, unblinking.

My heart broke when a tear slipped from her eyes.

"Sweetheart, don't cry…" A wiped the lone tear with my thumb.

"What is wrong with you?" Hailey asked me, her eyes shone with a ferocity that took me by surprise.

"How could you just waltz into my life and turn my life upside down in the most jaw dropping, transforming way and act like you didn't do anything?"

"I'm sorry…" I whispered. "I know I could have been quieter about it."

"You don't know what you mean to me, Walter." She looked away. "I love you so much that it scares me."

"I guess that makes two of us." Came my reply and her frown grew into a smile once again.

We were completely blanketed in darkness now, with only the twinkling stars and the blinking city lights illuminating the night.

Hailey shut her eyes, inhaling deeply like she was savouring the moment.

"I could stay here forever…" she muttered.

"I could stay anywhere forever, as long as you're there." I kissed her cheek.

"Do you ever run out of lines?" Hailey questioned, peering into my face with genuine curiousity.

"How could I? Not when my muse is right here…" I tapped her nose and she giggled.

"Close your eyes." I said to Hailey. She eyed me suspiciously for a moment, before asking.

"What are you about to do?"

"You ask too many questions, woman. Just close your eyes."

As she let her eyelids flutter close, I turned on the light in my car, pulling out a rectangular box from the basket beside me. I inspected its content before flipping it open facing her.

"Open your eyes, Hailey."

She gasped, her eyes almost bulging out of its socket.

"Oh my gosh, Walter…"

"Hailey…" I whispered. "You know how much I love you and how much I want you to be in my life. This is why I'm officially asking you to be my girlfriend."

Her eyes moved from the content of the box to my pleading eyes and she nodded with all her might.

"Yes! A thousand times yes!" Hailey squealed, wrapping her arms around me.

I pulled out the diamond bracelet from the box, securing it around her left wrist.

"This is so beautiful…" She breathed in awe. "Must have cost a fortune…Aw, Walter…"

"Shhh…" I placed my finger in front of her lips. "You're worth a thousand times more, Hailey."

She closed the distance between us, our lips locking in a slow, agonizing kiss.

WALTER

Sweat clung to my forehead, even though the air-conditioner was on full blast. I haven't felt this tensed in a long time, not even when I had a million dollar contract at stake.

With sweaty, trembling fingers, I dialed the first number on my phone, listening for the reciever.

"Pick up, you idiot." I hissed, tapping my feet on the floor of the car. I exhaled in relief when I heard his voice.

"Yo, Walter!" Ezra's cheerful voice made me sigh in relief. "How are you, man?"

"Thank goodness, for the first time you picked up when I needed you." I exclaimed.

"Hey, what do you mean by that?" Ezra sounded offended, but he knew I was only telling the truth.

If you were dying and you needed someone to help you, don't call Ezra. You'd be drinking tea with the Grimm reaper before he returns your call.

"I'm on my way to see my girlfriend's family and…I feel like a teenager again."

"Hold on, so let me get this straight…" Ezra started, and a groan escaped from my lips. I knew what he was going to say and I honestly wasn't ready for a lecture.

"You're telling me that you can dive headfirst into a stakeholder's meeting but you can't face your girlfriend's family without help from your bestfriend?"

"That's besides the point." I deadpanned,

"Can you just…help me out here?"

"You know, I may not be good at keeping relationships, but one thing I'm good at is winning the heart of any parent."

Ezra said smugly, and now that I think about it, he was right. My mum adored Ezra. I had no idea what he did or said, but no day went by without her asking about him.

I hated it when Ezra was right.

"Are you just going to toot your horn or are you going to be useful to me right now?" I snapped, just about to end the call when Ezra's voice stopped me.

"Relax man, your so sensitive."

"So? Are you going to help me?" I asked and he sighed.

"Right, here's what you're going to do…" Ezra began and I paid close attention to every word. It all sounded like a bunch of gibberish to me, and after five minutes of listening I knew I'd had enough.

"So basically you're telling me that I have to turn into you to win the heart of Hailey's parents?" I said flatly.

"If that gets the job done, why not?" Ezra replied, and knowing Ezra, he probably had a stupid smirk on his face while he said that.

"Uh, you know what? You're right. No one does it like you and I don't think I'm cut out for this." I surrendered in defeat.

"You don't have to be cut out for it, Waltz…all you've got to do is to ease into it, like a robe."

"I don't get it, but thank you." I replied.

"Look man, the truth behind all of this facade is to be yourself." Ezra voiced with seriousness.

"If her parents don't like you for who you truly are then what's the use?"

"I guess you're right." I reluctantly agreed.

"I mean–I knew that before but hearing it from you was the confirmation I needed."

"It sure is." Said Ezra. "Now can I go back to my chess match? Reggie is getting impatient."

"Get out of here, Ezra." I chuckled, ending the call with a beep.

I sat quietly for the rest of the ride, thinking about my first meeting with Hailey's dad. She had mentioned that he wasn't quite smitten by me and that didn't help my growing anxiety.

I understood why he was worried though. I would be worried as well if my daughter showed up at my doorstep with an older man. All I had to do was to make my intentions clear and everything should go smoothly…right?

"Are you okay, Sir?" Thomas asked, his voice laced with concern.

"Yes I am…why?" I enquired, watching Thomas from the rear view mirror.

"You seemed to have zoned out for a moment." He pointed out.

"Well, thank you for your concern, Thomas." I acknowledged, turning my attention to the surburban neighborhood we drove past.

The closer we got, the harder my heart thumped within my chest and when Thomas finally came to a stop in front of the apartment, I knew there was no escaping this.

"It's going to be a walk in the park." I said to myself, stepping down from the car with a bouquet of flowers in my hand.

"Easy peasy lemon squeezy."

Was it just me or did the hallway suddenly grow longer with every step I took? At this point I felt like I was loosing my mind.

"Focus, Walter. Focus!" I said to myself, adjusting my shirt before landing a few knocks on the door.

The tension that followed was loud, and I didn't know how long to wait before I knocked again.

I raised my knuckles to the door once more, but before they could land on the door it cracked open.

My fears fizzled out the moment I set my eyes on Hailey.

"Hey." She breathed, trying to hide the smile that creeped on her lips but her eyes gave her away.

"Hey." I replied, handing her a bouquet of freshly picked flowers.

"Aw, Thank you." She cooed, taking a long whiff of the bouquet before hugging them closer to her chest.

"Come in, everyone is expecting you."

My ears rang as I replayed Hailey's last words.

Everyone is expecting you.

Who is everyone and why are they expecting me?

With brisk steps, I followed Hailey down the familar corridor which led to the living room. A woman with platinum braids stepped out of the kitchen and from the sea blue eyes I knew that was Hailey's mum.

"Oh, our guest is here already."

"Good evening Mrs. Hernandez." I greeted with a small bow.

"Aw, you can call me Martha. Nice to finally meet you son." Said Martha, leading us to the dining room where a platter of food was set.

Heavy footsteps soon followed drawing closer with every passing second. Hailey and I exchanged a look, and she squeezed my hand reassuringly.

A bulky figure appeared at the door way, and our eyes locked in a hard stare.

"Good evening Mr. Hernandez." I greeted, hand outstretched to shake his hand. The older man stared me down for a moment before taking my hand.

"Welcome Walter." He said curtly, walking away to take a seat at the table. Hailey and I followed behind, taking the empty seats across from each other.

"So I made some roasted chicken with some rice and curry sauce…"Said Martha. She started dishing the food into our plates as she spoke.

She was about to dish mine, and she paused, turning to me.

"You do eat meat, right?"

"Of course, thank you." I managed a smile.

The first few minutes were marked with awkward silence, except for the clinking and clattering of cutleries. This was going weirder than I expected, and the silence was tearing me apart but I maintained my composure, slowly munching on my food.

I had to give it to her, Martha knew how to cook! But somehow I knew I wasn't savouring the taste of the meal like I would have if I wasn't subjected to this social torture.

After several minutes of glancing awkwardly at each other, the old man cleared his throat.

"Walter…" He paused for a moment. "Walter Wolfhard, is it?"

"Yes Sir. It's Walter Wolfhard." I affirmed, pausing my meal to give him my attention.

"So what do you do?" He continued.

"I'm the CEO and founder of Wolfgate Innovations." I say upright,

"We are a tech company focused on coming up with creative, problem solving concepts for companies."

"Hmmmm…." He hummed, savouring the taste of the chicken in his mouth before speaking once again.

"That's pretty impressive."

"Yes Dad, it is." Hailey chipped in with excitement. "We've worked with really big companies and I've learned so much in three months; more than I ever imagined."

"Hailey is very hardworking, and she has championed some brilliant ideas for the company." I smiled at her and her cheeks turned red.

"I'm so proud of you my baby." Martha gushed, turning to me.

"She has always been obsessed with problem solving since she was a child and it feels great to see her doing so well at such a young age."

"Yes, she's a…bright young lady." Martha's last statement left a feeling of uneasiness in the pit of my stomach, one that even this delicious meal couldn't quell.

"Which is why I wonder; what such an experienced; man would see in a…young lady like Hailey." Mr. Hernandez began, leaning back on his chair.

"Am I right, Martha?"

"Dad…" Hailey gritted her teeth, sending him a glare from the corner of her eyes.

"It is one question I believe shouldn't be too hard for you to answer. Afterall, you're a problem solver. This should be easy."

I raised the napkin to my lips, wiping the corners before responding.

"You're right. I'm experienced, like you said."

Hailey looked worried but I flashed her a smile before I continued.

"I've travelled the world, seen women of different ethnicities and race, but that's what makes Hailey special."

All eyes were on me, listening attentively.

"She's like a light, Mr. Hernandez. Hailey walks into a room and the atmosphere lightens up."

I stare down at my half-eaten plate, letting my memories and experiences guide my words.

"As cliche as this is sounds, Hailey is unlike any girl I've ever met. She didn't walk into my life. It was a crash, loud and disturbing." I chuckled.

"At first we were sworn enemies, never seeing to come to a compromise but when we got to know each other…when I got to know her, I realized she was all I've been searching for and more."

Martha sniffed, wiping her eyes with the back of her hand but Mr. Hernandez just stared down on me, like he was trying to figure out if I was genuine or just some sweet-talker who wanted to take advantage of his daughter.

"Maybe you should add poetry to your list of skills." He said, running his eyes over me.

"You have your way with words, but that's all it is…words."

"Dad." Hailey finally spoke.

"Walter has made me experience love in ways that I never imagined. He cares about every detail of my life and he's always urging me on to be the best version of myself."

"I don't know, Hailey." Mr. Hernandez said, eying me warily. "They all do that at first you know."

"Then let me learn from my experience." Hailey replied. "If he ends up not being the one for me, I'd have learnt won't I?"

Mr. Hernandez was speechless, but his eyes hardened as they locked on mine.

"Well, if that's the path you decide to tread, I can't stop you. I can only guide you and offer my advice. It's up to you to take it or leave it."

"Honey…" Martha turned to Mr. Hernandez. "How about you open your heart and just…get to know him?"

I just sat there awkwardly, munching quietly on my dinner while listening to them talk about me like I wasn't there.

"Fine." Mr. Hernandez quietly replied, and Hailey's face lit up with excitement.

Martha glanced at me with a warm, reassuring smile on her lips, and I smiled back in return.

After the meal, we had a game night and we split into two teams. Mr. Hernandez and I teamed up against Hailey and Martha.

Our first game was monopoly and after winning the women thrice in a row, Mr. Hernandez pulled me into a hug.

"This man knows his stuff!" He bragged, and Hailey rolled her eyes.

"Yeah? Wasn't that the same man you couldn't stand two hours ago?"

Martha and I burst into laughter as Mr. Hernandez stepped away from me like I stung.

"That was in the past, Hailey. Just let it go." He murmured.

"And that is why we're going to switch teams for the next game." Hailey huffed, pulling me to her side.

"Now it's couple against couple."

"Bring it on!" Martha exclaimed, slamming the next board game at the center of the living room table.

The rest of the night was filled with shouts of victory and cries of defeat, and at the end of the day both teams were too tired for a tie breaker.

"Just so you know, we went easy on you." Mr. Hernandez said and we all laughed our hearts out, ending the night with some Karaoke and homemade cheesecake.

WALTER

$\mathcal{I}$ tiptoed out of bed, my eyes glued to the beautiful human sprawled out at the other end. Holding my breath was an extreme sport, and I successfully made it to the closet without rousing the sleeping beauty.

I grabbed the bouquet of flowers, chocolates and a suede box, craddling them in my hands as I tiptoed back to the bedroom.

"Alexa…" I whispered. "Play me 'Everlasting love' by Blakes and Finleys."

"Playing 'Everlasting love' by….Blakes and Finleys" The robotic voice of the virtual assistant responded.

Piano keys blasted through the speakers, followed by the soothing voice of Harley Blake. If there's one thing that is able to draw Hailey from the deepest sleep, that would be The Blakes and Finleys.

So I wasn't surprised when her eyes flung open, followed by a lazy grin.

"...They say time heals all wounds..." Hailey's sonorous morning voice crooned along with Harley and I swayed towards her, singing along.

"...so tell me what time does for an everlasting love?"

We chuckled at the disharmony of our voices, and I gently pulled her out of the bed, wrapping my free arm around her waist.

"Happy birthday to the girl who stole my heart right under my watch." I planted a kiss on her lips.

"You've brought so much light and beauty to my life, Hailey. More than you'll ever know."

"If you're trying to make me cry, it's working." Hailey wiped her eyes.

"I know I've told you a thousand times before, but l will keep saying it until I breathe my last breath." My thumb caressed her cheek, catching a lone tear that rolled down from her eye.

"I love you, Hailey Corey Hernandez."

She winced at the sound of her middle name, narrowing her eyes at me.

"Not the middle name."

"Well I love you, middle name and all." I stole another kiss from her lips and she scrunched up her nose.

"Ew, stinky." She teased, shoving my face away from hers.

"Ouch." I clung to my chest in feign hurt.

"But I love you…stinky and all." Hailey replied, pressing her lips on mine.

We spent the rest of the morning dancing to the entire Blakes and Finleys album, before we kicked off with the day.

I had an entire surprise party planned out, and watching her sweet, little oblivious face staring back at me as we ate breakfast made it even more worthwhile.

Hailey hasn't really celebrated a lot of special days, so I wanted to make this one memorable.

"I just got a email from Alistar." I said with a frown.

"We're having an emergency meeting by 12pm."

"Oh." Hailey replied, disappointment spelt all over her features. "And it can't be rescheduled?"

"I thought about that, and I had just emailed them about it." I shook my head.

"They insisted on today. Something about a faulty model that needed restructuring."

"Well, that sucks." She slouched.

"I'm so sorry baby." I took her hand in mine and she forced a smile.

"It's fine, I just…wanted to spend the day with my favorite person but now this…"

"I'll be here with you." I pinched her cheek and she giggled. "Dont worry, it's going to be a perfect day."

Hailey and I got ready in about an hour, and by the time we stepped out of the house, Thomas was already waiting upfront with the car.

"Let's get this over with…" She muttered to herself, right before we stepped into the car.

As we drove down the busy streets of Chicago, Hailey sat quietly beside me.

"Are you okay?" I asked.

"Mhhmmmm…" She nodded, but I could tell she was upset. What she didn't know was that Thomas made a detour and we were heading in another direction.

After several minutes, she looked out the window and that was when she noticed.

"Wait, shouldn't we have arrived by now?" Hailey asked, confused.

"Yeah, you're right." I replied. "But the meeting is at a different location."

"I guess that makes sense." She shrugged, resting her head on my shoulder.

"We've not even arrived yet and I'm already tired." Hailey sighed.

"I know…" I gently ran my hands through her loose curls. "Or do you want to go back home? You don't have to come."

"I want to be with you, Walter." Hailey said, planting a kiss on my neck.

"And I love having you around." I kissed her hair.

We fell back into comfortable silence, until Thomas parked in front of a magnificent penthouse.

"We're here." I whispered to Hailey and she looked around the unfamiliar environment.

"What is this place?" Her eyes darted about with curiosity.

"Let's find out, shall we?" I stretched out my hand and Hailey eyed it with suspicion.

"Trust me, Hailey Hernandez."

She placed her hand in mine and together we stepped out of the car, walking into the building.

An attendant walked up to us with a warm smile.

"Welcome Sir and ma'am, this way please."

We were led to a beauty hub first and Hailey turned to me, confused.

"This is the meeting with Alistar? A full body spa session?"

I acted aloof, raising my shoulders in a nonchalant shrug.

"I'm as shocked as you are."

"You're such a terrible liar." She chuckled, walking into the room.

Her session was going to last for three hours, so I had enough time to find out how far preparations were going and monitor their progress.

What felt like such a long time soon ran out, and I got a call from Hailey that she was all done.

I stepped into the room and my jaws hit the floor when she stepped out.

Her tan skin glistened under the glowing light, and her silky hair fell in cascading locks. Her golden dress sparkled under the light, hugging every inch of her perfect curves. She was a sight to behold, and in that moment I couldn't form any words.

"So…what do you think?" she asked,

"Breathtaking." I muttered. "You are breathtaking, Hailey Hernandez."

"Thank you." She curtsied. "You tricked me, you know."

I pulled her into my arms, pressing a kiss on her forehead.

"And I would do it again just to see that look on your face."

We left afterwards, and despite her please I refused to disclose our next location. She didn't seem to happy about that, her lips curled into an angry pout.

"My cute little angry bird." I tapped her nose and she swatted my hand.

"I'll get you for this."

"I'd like to see you try." I replied, suppressing a smile.

Soon we were riding up a hill and Hailey's face lit up.

"No way." She looked out the window. "No freaking way."

Thomas slowed down, parking in front of a familar cabin in the outskirts of town.

Before Thomas killed the engine, Hailey had jumped out of the car, racing down to the cabin.

"Shit…" I cussed, following her behind. Man, could she run and she flung the door open.

I had no idea what she was expecting, but the smile on her face faded when the lights didn't come on.

She turned to me, confused but I only smiled. That seemed to infuriate her, but before she could say a word, the sound of guitar strings interrupted her tirade.

Her hands flew to her mouth, watching as the six members of the Blakes and Finleys appeared out of the darkness.

"This is for you, birthday girl." Oscar Finley said, strumming his guitar as they harmonized one of Hailey's favorite song.

The girl I found.

As they sang, flash lights began to flicker and soon it felt like the stars were trapped in the house with us.

Only that these stars were the people Hailey loved.

"Mum…dad…" She croaked, tears rolling down her face uncontrollably.

"Stacey? What are you doing here? Oh my gosh, everyone is here!"

They all surrounded her, singing along with the Blakes and Finleys. As the song came to an end, the lights came on, followed by a rain of confetti.

"Happy Birthday Hailey!"

My baby girl was a sobbing mess, unable to hold back the emotions that overcame her. It was such a beautiful sight and my heart swelled with pride that I was able to make this happen for her.

Hailey was a bubbly angel for the rest of the party, dancing, singing and laughing all night. After the toast, Hailey's dad walked up to me.

"You see this thing you did?" He gestured at the party. "Hailey is never going to forget it."

I nodded with a smile, clinking glasses with the old man.

"I'm sorry I doubted you, Walter." He confessed. "You're a good man, and I'm happy my daughter ended up with such an amazing person."

"I appreciate your kind words, Mr. Hernandez." I said to him, before going to meet Martha who beckoned us to join Hailey for some pictures.

HAILEY

It was early in the morning, and the birds were still asleep except the rooster whose cry tore through the quiet of the darkness.

I laid there in my bed, shrouded in the dark with just a little lamp which illuminated the pages I was scribbling on. My life has changed so much in six months, more than I ever imagined.

Now that I was leaving for college, I didn't know what awaited me on this new path. My life's journey has always been marked with unpredictability. No matter how hard I tried to force things to fit my plans, fate seemed to have something better in store for me but this time, I was prepared.

At least I thought I was.

Still, fear clung to me like a leech, feeding off my uncertainty. But I knew it was okay to be afraid.

I slammed my journal shut, curling up into a ball as I thought about the journey that lay ahead of me. My eyes strayed to my well-arranged luggage which sat at the corner of my room and my heart ached.

I was going to be living my dreams of studying software engineering in the University of Wales, but I was also going to be leaving a lot of beautiful memories and people behind.

I was leaving Walter behind.

Tears escaped from my eyes at the thought of being apart from him, wishing there was a way we could bridge the distance.

"You will figure it out, Hailey. You always will." I muttered to myself before I drifted back to sleep.

I woke up a few hours later to my alarm, dragging myself to the shower. I knew I had to get ready on time, if I didn't want to miss my flight. I slipped on a pair of cargo pants and a hoody, letting my curls run wild and free.

"Are you ready to go?"

Walter leaned at the door frame at the entrance of my room, trying to hide the sadness in his eyes with a smile.

"Yeah." I nodded, bobbing my head towards my packed luggage.

"Thomas is waiting outside." Walter mentioned quietly. And I nodded again. He walked into the room.

"What's on your mind?" Walter asked, his eyes scrutinizing every inch of my face.

"I'm scared." I confessed. "I'm scared of what this new phase holds for me. For us. I don't want to be away from you."

"Oh, my love." Walter's voice broke, wrapping his arms around me. I drank in his citrus scent, relishing in the feeling of his arms around me. He cupped my face in his hand, his eyes burning with intensity.

"Our love is stronger than the chasm of distance, Hailey. We will get through this."

"Or I can stay here and work with you…at Wolfgate." I suggested and Walter chuckled.

"And let you give up on your dreams? Not on my watch." He shook his head.

"I promised your dad I would support your dream and that is what I'm going to do."

My eyes watered and a smile spread across my lips.

"I love you so much, Walter Wolfhard."

He pressed his forehead against mine, his breath ragged with emotion.

"I love you with all my heart, Hailey Hernandez."

Our lips locked in a feverish kiss, slow and agonizing. Tears slipped from my eyes as it grew more intense and fiery like it was our last.

My fingers found there way to his curls, holding on to it for dear life as his lips devoured mine.

I fell into his arms afterwards and I knew I'd found my home. And the thing about home is that no matter how far you go, you will always come back home.

About the Author

J. D. Hova is an author who perfectly blends passion, hope, and real-life meanings in his romance books. When he is not writing, you can find him enjoying the great outdoors with his family, dogs, chickens, and new-born baby. J. D. believes that true love and happiness take time and his books reflect that belief. His stories capture the essence of life and offer a glimmer of hope through happy ever afters. If you enjoyed reading his books, please leave a review as he truly appreciates your feedback.

Acknowledgments

I want to take a moment to express my sincerest gratitude to all the amazing people in my life. Without the love and support of my readers, friends, family, and colleagues, I wouldn't be where I am today. I am so grateful for each and every one of you who has helped me along my path to happiness and success. I also want to give a special shoutout to those who hold me accountable and contribute so much to making this journey through life possible. And of course, I can't forget to thank the most important women who has inspired me – Linda V., my sweet baby girl Ayla, Grand Mother Louise, Mother Kathy, Sister Shannon and Aunt Christine. Thank you all from the bottom of my heart.